A Cowboy and his Fake Marriage

A Johnson Brothers Novel, Chestnut Ranch Romance, Book 6

Emmy Eugene

ISBN-13: 979-8630701459

CHAPTER 1

Darren Dumond liked the quiet stillness of the ranch early in the morning. He'd just come in from feeding the horses, and he needed to hurry. He took a moment on the back porch though, as if waiting for his new golden retriever puppy to bobble his way up the steps.

But Koda had already made it to the door and he panted, waiting for Darren to open the door. He took one last look out over the land, the bubbling of the river barely audible in the distance. He breathed in deeply, because he needed today to be a good day.

"It's going to be great," he told himself. "Rex is getting married, and I have a new suit to wear." He bent down and ruffled the dog's ears. "Even you have a bow tie, bud. Let's go get ready."

He opened the door then and went inside, repeating the words, "It's going to be a great day," over and over.

He desperately needed it to be, because he hated weddings with the heat of a thousand suns. But he couldn't just not show up. He was friends with Rex, and the man had asked Darren to be in the wedding party.

Griffin was the best man, and he'd gotten engaged a few days ago too, when the Johnson parents had returned from their service mission to the Dominican Republic.

Darren blinked, and he saw Conrad Johnson lying on the ground, his leg bent unnaturally underneath him. Panic reared, and everything that had happened after Darren had found the man thrown from his horse streamed through his mind.

Conrad was an experienced horseman, but the horse he'd been working with was young, and unbroken, and wild. Conrad couldn't remember what had happened to spook the horse, but Darren had found it running free on the ranch and known immediately that something was wrong.

Conrad had never walked the same again, and he couldn't ride anymore. Darren's compassion for the man had doubled as he watched him fight for every inch of mobility he had, and he wasn't too tough of a cowboy to say he'd shed a few tears the day Conrad and Sally had left the ranch for a single-level home in the center of Chestnut Springs.

Then he could get to his doctor's appointments quicker, and the grocery store was closer. Life was just easier when they didn't have to drive fifteen to twenty minutes for everything, especially as Conrad couldn't drive anymore.

So much had been taken from him in just a split second,

and Darren understood exactly how that felt. He'd lost everything he cherished in the same amount of time, and he was still reeling and trying to figure things out.

Which was why he'd had to break-up with Sarena Adams. He couldn't shake the feelings of infidelity he had, though Diana had been gone for a long time now.

He sighed as he soaped up, wishing the negative thoughts and emotions swirling inside him could wash down the drain as easily as the suds.

"It's a good day," he told himself as he tipped his head back into the shower spray. "I have hot water."

As he continued getting ready, he named all of his blessings. "The cabin has air conditioning."

"I have an amazing pup." He grinned at Koda as he got the dog dressed for the wedding. "And good friends."

He thought of the family he'd left years ago, and he determined he'd call his mother that night. Maybe if he talked to her, she could help him see how unreasonable he was being.

The thing was, he *knew* he was being unreasonable. But he couldn't rid himself of the feelings. But his mother had a way of saying things in a way that Darren hadn't thought about before, and maybe...

He held onto maybe's these days like they were anchors. He needed some of them to be true.

Maybe he could have another loving relationship with a woman.

Maybe he could tell Sarena about Diana.

Maybe he could be happy again.

He bent down to leash Koda when Aaron came in the back door. "You two ready?" the other cowboy asked.

"So ready." Darren stood up smiling, sure of one thing: He could smile through this day. *It's going to be a great day...*

AN HOUR LATER, he held the leash loosely in his hand as he waited for the ceremony to start. Holly and Rex had wanted to get married in their backyard, and Rex had hired Millie to make it look like paradise.

A huge tent filled almost the whole thing, with lights and flowers hanging from the ceiling. Chairs had been set up inside, and Millie bustled around straightening the bows and reserving seats as the first guests started to arrive.

Darren told himself it was almost over, because he knew Rex had given Holly what she wanted—a simple ceremony with just family and very close friends.

So he was more than surprised to see Sarena Adams enter the backyard through the gate, both of her sisters with her. She wore a long, pale pink dress that brushed the grass and made it impossible for Darren to know if she was wearing shoes or not.

The sight of her almost made it impossible for Darren to breathe. She was gorgeous, with the dress swelling in all the right places and tying around her neck, leaving her shoulders and some of her back bare.

She stepped right over to Janelle, Russ's wife, and hugged her hello. All the sisters did, and then they looked around for a place to sit. At least that was what Darren thought initially. But he soon realized they were looking for someone.

As all four of them continued to whisper and search, Darren watched Sarena. Kissing her had reintroduced magic into his life. Holding her hand reminded him that he wasn't alone in this world, even if he had put up some walls to keep people out. She'd started to break those walls down, and he'd let her.

They'd dated until about a week ago, when he'd told her he wasn't sure he could do more than be friends with a woman. She'd wanted to know what that meant, and he had no explanation. She'd said he didn't kiss her like they were friends, and he couldn't argue with her.

He had not told her about Diana, and even now his tongue felt too thick inside his mouth. He'd only told two people about his late wife—Griffin and Conrad Johnson. And he'd only told Griffin because the man had come across Darren while he was looking at his wedding pictures on his phone—and crying.

Griffin had been nothing but kind and compassionate, and as far as Darren knew, he'd never told anyone about Diana.

Darren's heart pulsed too many times, too closely together, and that somehow made Sarena look in his direction. She froze, her eyes widening. Janelle said something to her, but Sarena didn't even react.

Janelle was one of the smartest women Darren knew, and she followed Sarena's frozen gaze. Her eyes landed on Darren too, and she stared at him for a moment as well. Then she stepped in front of Sarena, breaking their connection.

Darren cleared his throat and ducked his head, his face heating quickly. "We're ready for you and Koda," someone said, and he turned toward Travis. He'd been keeping an eye on his pregnant wife and helping with the setup, so Darren followed him back into the house.

Rex stood there, and he looked more agitated than usual. Travis said, "Okay, we're ready to get Rex out there. Momma you come too." He looked around. "Where did Millie go?"

"Right here," she said, panting as she bustled into the house. "The seats are almost full. Let's get the family out there. If you're in the wedding party, you stay right here. Griffin, you're going to lead them down the steps and escort a lady down the aisle. The women are waiting at the bottom of the steps."

Griffin nodded and smiled. "We practiced this, Millie. We've got it."

"And Seth's back with Holly?"

"I sent him back a few minutes ago," Travis said.

Millie nodded and looked around at the crowd. "Okay, everyone knows what to do. Rex, you're with me." She took the groom with her, and they went outside. Darren waited in the dining room, the scent of frosting and rose petals floating in the air.

Everything was happening right here at the house. First, Rex and Holly would be married. Re-married, technically. Then they were serving lunch, and Darren had volunteered to move chairs and help set up tables in the same space under the tent.

After they cut their cake, they'd leave on a honeymoon,

something they'd never done when they'd gotten married the first time. Rex had wanted to go big with the wedding, Darren knew, but he was secretly on Holly's side.

Smaller was always better, and if he ever got married again, he'd want it to be a private ceremony with just him and his bride. Maybe her family, if she wanted them there. And probably the Johnsons, as they'd done so much for Darren over the past four years.

His thoughts migrated right to Sarena, but he told himself that was because she was the only woman he'd been out with since Diana's death. He thought about her as he took his place in line. As the excitement mounted as they went down the steps. As he linked arms with Jenna Johnson, Seth's wife, and kept Koda at his side. People pointed and smiled at the dog, and pride swelled within Darren.

He smiled through it all, and he steadfastly watched the woman dominating his thoughts. The ceremony was short and simple, but absolutely beautiful.

"I will love you forever," Rex said, his voice catching on itself. "I've never stopped loving you, and I'm glad to be yours."

Darren had never stopped loving Diana either, and he didn't think it was fair to Sarena to not give her his whole heart. Surely she understood that and didn't even want someone who couldn't give her everything. Right?

He cheered and clapped when Rex and Holly kissed, and he helped set up tables like he'd agreed to do. Lunch was served, and he lost track of Sarena. Maybe she and her sisters hadn't stayed for lunch.

He let Koda roam the yard with Holly's dog, and he stuck close to Aaron, Brian, and Tomas as they got their food and found a table. He'd barely taken a bite of his rosemary chicken when someone sat beside him.

The scent of the woman pricked his attention. He didn't have to look to know Sarena had just sat next to him. "Is this seat taken?"

"No, ma'am," he muttered, twisting his shoulders slightly so he was turned further away from her.

She didn't say anything else, but her sisters started talking about the ceremony and how perfect Rex and Holly were for each other. The chicken stuck in Darren's throat. He couldn't sit here like this.

This was torture.

Absolute torture.

He got up and took his plate with him.

"Hey," Aaron said. "Where are you—?"

But Darren walked away before he could finish. He couldn't breathe. He couldn't swallow. He hurried up the steps, almost knocking down a waiter in his haste to get out of Sarena's sight.

He burst into the house, sucking at the air. He'd felt this wild and out of control just once before, and that was the day he'd buried Diana. He waited for the episode to pass, but when it did, he was left sweating and exhausted.

Thankfully, it only took a few seconds too, and he thought maybe he could make an excuse about needing to use the restroom. The house was quiet while the yard was noisy, and it seemed like everyone had been served now.

He put his plate on the counter near the sink and turned, trying to decide where to go.

Sarena stepped into the house, locking the door behind her. "Darren," she said. "I know you broke up with me. I don't understand why, and I just have to say this. Then you can decide what you want to do."

She pressed her palms together and looked over her shoulder. When her eyes came back to his, she looked nervous yet hopeful.

"I really like you," she said, her voice throaty and oh-so-sexy. "I don't know why you don't...no, that's not what I want to say." She drew in a deep breath and steadied herself. "I want you to know that you can trust me."

She looked like she might say something more, but she just nodded. "That's it. You can trust me with anything." She took a step toward him. "Your secrets. Your past. Your hopes and dreams and future." She moved with every item she said, and soon she was only a couple of feet from him.

She reached out and touched his chest, right over his heart. A shock moved through his body, and she whispered, "Your heart." She looked up at him. "Okay?"

He nodded as an automatic response, but he couldn't get his voice to work.

She nodded too, and with those beautiful eyes sparkling at him with need and desire and hope, she tipped up on her toes and swept a kiss along his cheek. "Okay."

With that, she turned and left the way she'd come. The door opened, letting in the noise from outside, and the moment between them broke.

She left, and Darren couldn't breathe again.

She left, and Darren's world didn't make sense anymore.

She left, and Darren immediately wanted her back.

He just didn't know how to have her and Diana at the same time.

CHAPTER 2

"Maybe I should go," Sorrell said.

"We're all going," Sarena said as she plucked another errant eyebrow hair from her brow line. "Why aren't you dressed yet?"

"I really thought you talking to Darren would work." Sorrell wrapped her arms around herself, her nerves pouring from her expression.

Sarena had thought that too. But in the two weeks since Rex Johnson's wedding, he had not called her. She'd walked out to the back fence every morning and every night, and he did not come. The notes she left for him there had not been picked up.

He'd gotten a puppy, and maybe that was all he needed in his life. Puppies were easy to talk to. Puppies were warm at night.

But Sarena didn't want a puppy. She wanted Darren back

in her life—and not just because her time to tie the knot or lose the ranch was dwindling.

But it was, and that was why she was going to the speed dating event during the town's Octoberfest tonight.

And Sorrell should be as well, but one more glance at her sister, and Sarena knew she wouldn't be going.

She'd told her sisters about the stipulation in their father's will the same day Darren had broken up with her. They'd immediately started brainstorming other men any of the three of them could go out with, but the choices were slim.

It had only taken an hour for them to come back to Darren, and they'd started devising a plan for Sarena to get him back.

But the relationship was about more than the ranch, and she knew it. Sorrell and Serendipity didn't need to know.

And he hadn't called. She couldn't make him call.

So while her heart continued to beat, it was a shell of what it had once been. Without him, Sarena didn't feel half as alive, and she doubted that she'd ever be able to be her authentic self with someone.

The worst part was how lonely she was. She sighed as she finished her makeup and smiled as Sorrell helped her into her dress. "You're going to get a ton of dates," Sorrell said. "You don't need me to come."

"I knew you wouldn't." Sarena smiled at her sister. She'd always known it would be her that would get married to save the ranch.

She just needed to find someone.

Tonight, she told herself. She was going to find someone

tonight. Janelle had become a good friend over the past three months, and she said Jenna and Seth had started dating in the fall and been married by Thanksgiving, so it was definitely doable.

Armed with that hope, Sarena drove herself to town and parked in the community center parking lot. Though it was October, it certainly wasn't cold in the Hill Country, and she hoped her boots wouldn't be too noticeable.

She'd never told Darren about her prosthetic foot, and she was glad about that. She didn't need his pity on top of the other humiliation.

She'd arrived early, and the men were still getting instructions and going through the set up. She waited with the other women in the room, quickly realizing that all of them were hoping for the same thing she was—a wedding by Christmas.

Her stomach revolted, and she almost bolted from the room. But there were easily sixty or seventy men here, most of them wearing cowboy hats. She needed to meet someone if she was going to get married, and there weren't a lot of men knocking on the door at Fox Hollow.

She steeled herself as the emcee got behind the mic. "And we're ready. Ladies, you were given a number when you got here. You'll start at the table with the matching number, and we'll start the clock in five minutes." She smiled down at everyone from the small stage at the end of the room. "Everyone grab a drink and get ready to talk! The rounds are three minutes, and we hope you'll make some great connections tonight. You'll go in ascending order, with table seventy-six rotating to number one."

Sarena was hoping for that too. She'd brought a tiny purse with her driver's license, a credit card, her phone, and a couple of mints. She put one in her mouth, took a bottle of water from the table, skipping the coffee and sweet tea, and faced the sea of tables where the men waited.

After a quick glance, she started looking for table sixty-five. She caught the eyes of several men as she wove through the tables, and she earned herself more than one smile. She started to relax before she'd even reached the sixty row.

Maybe this would work.

She almost tripped when she saw Darren's face. One of her feet stopped, and the fake one kept going, and she had to steady herself against the nearest table, which was number fifty-one.

Darren sat at fifty-seven.

She wouldn't make it to him during the speed dating.

His eyes wouldn't leave hers, even when his first date sat down in front of him and introduced herself.

Sarena wondered what in the world he'd been thinking when he'd broken up with her. The spark and chemistry between them was insanely hot and powerful. Could he not feel it? Did he not care?

And now he was here?

Hurt and humiliation flooded her throat, and Sarena gagged against it.

"Are you okay?" someone asked—the man whose table she still used to support herself. He stood up and put one hand on her back and the other on her forearm. He said something else she didn't catch, because when she and Darren were in a room together, he was the only one she could see and hear.

So he just didn't like *her*. He didn't want to be more than friends with *her*.

For a week or two after he'd broken up with her, she'd reasoned that he just wasn't ready. He'd told her that he hadn't dated in a long time, and that was the best reason she could come up with by herself.

But he was here. So he obviously thought he was ready.

He just doesn't like you.

Sarena couldn't see straight, and thankfully, the cowboy from table fifty-whatever had helped her to a seat along the side of the room and opened her bottle of water for her. She drank with a shaky hand. The emcee chirped into the mic. The room spun.

Everything hurt, and while Sarena knew her time was running out, and she desperately needed to meet someone soon, she couldn't stay here. Not with *him* here.

She stood, glad her feet supported her, and headed for the exit. She'd suffered enough humiliation at the hands of Darren Dumond. She reached the doors and went through them. Just across the lobby, freedom lay.

She wanted to run, but she wasn't great on her feet when she moved too fast. So she settled for walking.

"Sarena," a man called behind her, but the sound of Darren's voice only spurred her to go faster. Tears streamed down her face now, and she would *not* let him see her like this. He would not get the satisfaction of knowing that he'd broken her heart all over again.

She burst through the doors, taking huge gulps of air, and kept on going.

You're being ridiculous, she told herself.

She was stronger than some cowboy who'd kissed her a few times. Though, she knew it was a lot more than a few times, and that each time Darren had touched her, she'd felt cherished and alive in a way she'd never felt before.

She'd been running the ranch nearly single-handedly for over five years. She could handle a little heartbreak.

"Sarena," he said again, and he was much closer now.

Sarena broke into a stilted jog, her right leg throbbing with the effort it took to keep the left one from buckling. She knew the moment she was going to fall, and she flailed her arms out, trying to find something to latch onto.

Only open air met her fingers, and she twisted to land on her hip.

"Sarena." Darren reached her a moment later. "I'm sorry. I'm sorry." He put those big, warm hands on her arms, his eyes searching for where she was hurt. But he couldn't see through skin and bone to her wounded heart beneath her ribs.

"You're bleeding." He touched her knee, and Sarena winced. "Where else does it hurt?"

Everywhere, she thought. Just having him so close was like the most brutal form of torture she could imagine.

He met her eyes. "I'm sorry," he said again. "Let me take you home and get you fixed up."

She shook her head, swallowing her emotion. "No," she said. "You should go back inside. You're going to miss all of your dates."

He gazed at her again, so many things streaming through those dark, deep eyes. "I don't care," he finally said. "I don't want to go out with any of them anyway." And with that, he picked her up and started toward his truck.

"Darren," she protested, though it sure was nice to be in his arms again. "I have my own truck."

"We'll come back." He wasn't taking no for an answer, and Sarena didn't want to give him those two letters anyway.

"You don't have to do this," she said as he set her on the bench seat in his truck.

"I have a first aid kit right here," he said, opening the glove box. He looked at her again. "And I want to do this." He stilled, and the whole world fell away. "I trust you, Sarena."

Those stupid tears filled her eyes again, and she brushed them away quickly. "You didn't call."

His throat worked, and then he opened the first aid kit and got busy looking at her scraped knees. He cleaned them up and put a couple of Band-Aids on them. "What else hurts?" he asked.

She didn't answer, because she didn't want to tell him all of her secrets. *She* didn't trust *him*, at least not yet.

But she didn't have much time, she knew that.

She reached down and touched her left ankle, her fingers meeting the hard plastic of her prosthetic through her sock. "Here," she said, her voice hardly her own. "And here." She touched her own chest, just above her heart.

Surprise filled Darren's expression, but it was quickly overtaken by something softer and then more anguished. "I've made a huge mess of things, haven't I?" He ducked his head, which was just adorable. He'd done it many times over the last few months they'd been seeing each other, and he usually did it when he was embarrassed or scared.

Which was he right now?

Probably both, Sarena reasoned.

"I miss you," she said, employing her bravery.

He lifted his eyes to hers. "I miss you, too."

"Why are you here?" She gestured toward the community center and the speed dating.

"I—I—" He cleared his throat and swallowed hard, but he didn't look away from her. "I think I'm ready, Sarena."

"But you just don't want to go out with me."

"I do," he said. "You're the *only* person I want to go out with."

"Then *why* are you *here*?" She didn't understand, and she really just wanted to stop thinking about him.

"Because I was too embarrassed to call you."

Sarena searched his face, trying to find any evidence of a lie. But Darren was as humble as he was handsome, and she wasn't even sure the man knew how to lie. Her foot ached, and she really needed to adjust it. She reached down and said, "Okay, listen, I have to fix this, and I don't want you to freak out."

"Freak out?"

She didn't answer as she took off her ankle boot and sock. "I have a prosthetic foot." She stuck her fingers between the silicon and her skin, breaking the seal there. A sigh escaped her lips when the false part of her foot released, and she took it all the way off.

"I was in an accident about ten years ago," she said as Darren fell back a step. "And I crushed the bones in my foot. We were able to save the ankle and some of the heel, and now I wear this."

Darren looked at the prosthetic in her hand and then looked at her. "Wow, Sarena." He wore compassion in his eyes. "Do you—can I help you with it?"

"No, I just don't run well, and I need to adjust it." She made quick work of getting the prosthetic back where it should be, covering it with her sock and then her boot. "All good."

But she'd exposed herself completely to him, and she wondered if he knew that. From the wide-eyed look on this face, he did.

The silence stretched between them, and Sarena knew to simply let it. Darren was a brilliant man, hardworking and kind. But he tended to take a while to order his thoughts before they came out of his mouth.

"I need to tell you something," he finally said. He took a step closer to her, filling the space between where she sat on the seat and the open passenger door.

"Okay," she prompted when he didn't say anything.

"I broke up with you, because my feelings for you were starting to get out of control." He swallowed, but his words made Sarena feel like singing praises to the sky. "See, I've been...married before, and I lost my wife five years ago."

"Oh, no," Sarena said, reaching out and cradling his face in her palm. He leaned into her touch, and the moment between them was so sweet.

"I didn't mean to hurt you," he whispered. "I felt disloyal to her, and my knee jerk reaction was to break-up with you."

Sarena just looked at him, this handsome man she wanted to spend more time with. "But you think you're ready now?"

"I honestly don't know," he said. "So this is probably really selfish of me, but would you like to go to dinner with me?"

"Right now?"

A slow smile crossed his face. "Yeah, right now."

Sarena couldn't think of anything better in the whole world, so she said, "Yeah, I'd like to go to dinner with you."

"Great." His smile turned into a full cowboy grin, and he leaned toward her as if he'd kiss her.

She sucked in a breath and froze, and Darren did too. "I guess...uh...yeah, let's start with dinner." He backed out of the doorway, and she turned so she was sitting in the seat the right way. He closed the door and started around the hood of the truck, muttering to himself.

Sarena smiled and tucked her hair, because Darren Dumond had almost kissed her. She was going to dinner with him. And maybe, just maybe, they could pick up where they'd left off a month ago.

She hoped so, because the clock was ticking.

CHAPTER 3

Now that Darren had Sarena in his truck, he didn't know what to do with her. Thankfully, he'd been driving for over twenty years, and he could do that without having to think too hard. He knew Sarena liked the Thanksgiving dinner pot pie at PotPied, and he could literally eat anything off their menu, so he turned toward the downtown area.

With the truck moving in a relatively straight line down the road, he cut a glance at Sarena. "I'm sorry about the...thing in there." He'd seen her face go completely white, watched her throw her hand out to support herself, and stood up when that other man had helped her to a chair on the side of the room.

He'd been so stupid not to call her.

"I told you you could trust me," Sarena said, her voice quiet and filling the feminine hold that existed in Darren's soul.

He nodded, his fingers too tight on the steering wheel. He made a conscious effort to loosen them, trying to get the lump in his throat to break up too. "I know," he said. "I trust you, Sarena. It's me I don't trust."

"Tell me more about that," she said.

Frustration continued to build in his chest. "I just...don't want to hurt you while I figure things out for myself."

"I'm willing to go on that ride," Sarena said. "Okay, Darren? I'm willing to be there while you do that."

Darren was sure she had no idea what she was really saying. "It could take a long time."

"Ah, see, I don't have a lot of that," Sarena said, causing Darren to look at her again.

"What do you mean?"

"Can I tell you later?"

Darren didn't know how to tell her no, so he said, "Sure, I guess."

She gave him one of the sexy smiles he'd missed so much. He could see her sitting on top of the fence so clearly, and hear her tell him she hadn't pegged him for a liar because his driver's license had the wrong weight on it.

He'd just pulled into the parking lot at PotPied when she asked, "When you say you 'lost' your wife, what did you mean by that?"

His heart shot to the top of his skull and then rebounded back to its rightful place in his chest. He looked left, away from her, and turned into a parking spot. "She died."

"I'm so sorry," Sarena said.

"Thank you," he said, his automatic response when people

found out about Diana and they apologized, as if they'd been responsible for her death.

"Any kids?"

"Nope."

"Where are you from?"

"Frio," he said. "Diana was from Hondo. She's buried there." The words didn't sting his throat as much as he'd thought they would. "We had a ranch down there for a couple of years, but I sold it after she died." He finally swung his attention toward Sarena, who gazed fully at him with those shiny, dark eyes that glinted like so much gold at midnight.

"Now you work at Chestnut Ranch."

"That's right," he said. "And I'm starving, and if they're out of the tri-tip pot pie, I might do...I don't know what. Something really bad."

Sarena blinked at him, and then burst out laughing. "Well, we can't have that. Come on, cowboy. Let's start praying they have that tri-tip pie so you don't have to 'do something really bad.'" She giggled again, and Darren sure did like the sound of it. It sank right into his ears and reminded him of how much he liked having this woman in his life.

He couldn't believe he'd broken up with her. Or that he hadn't called her back. He did take a moment to send up a quick prayer while he got out of the truck and walked around the front of it.

The only thought he had was to push his stubbornness aside, and he wondered what that looked like for him. He didn't consider himself to be particularly stubborn, but the moment he reached for Sarena's door handle, he reminded himself that he hadn't called her after she'd talked to him at Rex's wedding.

Why hadn't he done that?

He'd been too stubborn.

Sarena turned toward him and took his hand as he offered it to her. She slid from the truck in her skinny jeans, and Darren drank in the length of her legs and the beauty of her face.

"You look amazing tonight," he said, tucking her hand in his and keeping her at his side.

"I had to get all cleaned up for the speed dating," she said. "Both of my sisters helped me."

"Did either of them come?"

"No," Sarena said slowly. "We decided I would be the one to try the speed dating."

Darren looked at her, trying to understand more than what she'd said out loud. "I don't get it," he said. "Couldn't you have all come? There were a lot of men there." More than Darren had thought there would be, but Griffin had assured him a lot of adults would be present at the annual Octoberfest speed dating event.

"We...sort of have a pressing need," she said.

"A need for what?" he asked.

"I'm going to have to tell you," she said, and when she cast him a look, her eyes had filled with nerves. "But can we eat first?"

"Okay," Darren said. He'd left his cabin that evening, knowing he'd probably have to be patient. He'd definitely have to make a lot of small talk, as well as talk to women he didn't particularly want to talk to.

He reminded himself that he *wanted* to talk to Sarena—that conversing with her had been all he'd been thinking about for three weeks now—and he asked, "How'd things go with that troublesome hog?"

"Oh, my goodness," she said, tipping her head back and making all her dark curls spill down over her shoulders. "He broke through that fence four more times until I threatened to turn him into bacon. Somehow, he understood that, and he didn't do it again." She gave him a highly flirtatious look. "Well, that, and I called a fencing expert, and he reinforced the entire bottom half of the fence. Boris would have to be made of cement to get through it, but that didn't stop him from trying."

"Who'd you call?"

"Nick Ridley."

"He's good," Darren said. "I'm glad he helped you." He would've liked to have been the one to help her, but his own stubbornness had prevented that.

"What about you?" she asked. "Things humming along at Chestnut Ranch?"

"Yeah," he said. "Yep. Humming right along."

"How's the puppy?"

Darren smiled despite himself. He loved the little golden retriever, and he hated kenneling him while he went out. He took the dog to work with him, and the only time Koda had to sit in the kennel was if Darren left the cabin in the evening.

So really, hardly ever.

"He must be great," Sarena said. "You're smiling like a fool."

Darren supposed he was, and he couldn't straighten his mouth. "Yeah, he's great. Smart as anything. Loves to train and work."

"Sounds like Louisville."

"Well, I don't think Koda came from a championship line of racehorses," Darren said. He'd never met her horse, but Sarena had told him plenty about the sorrel and how amazing he was. She clearly loved the horse as much as Darren now loved his dog.

He put his hand on Sarena's lower back, guiding her to the register as it became their turn to order. "I'll have the Thanksgiving Feast," she said. "And do you have the Triple Threat?"

"Yes, ma'am," the teenager there said with entirely too much enthusiasm.

"Great." Sarena smiled on back at her. "We'll take that too."

"To stay or to go?"

"To stay," Darren said, removing his wallet from his back pocket. "And two drinks. And one of those chocolate pots." He looked a Sarena. "Do you want the peach pot pie?"

"Yes."

"And a peach pot pie," he added.

The girl repeated it all back to him, and Darren nodded as he extended his card toward her. Sarena went to choose a table while Darren went to the soda machine to fill their drinks.

As he sat across from her, he said, "Sprite, with a little splash of lemonade."

"Just how I like it." She reached for one of the straws he tossed on the table.

PotPied had fast service, and Darren had barely put his own straw in his cup and settled at the table when the food arrived. Things stayed light through dinner, and Darren couldn't believe he'd intentionally deprived himself of spending time with this woman.

He held her hand on the way back to his truck. "Back to the community center?" he asked as he reached to open her door for her.

Sarena turned toward him and stepped into his arms. "You can take me to get my truck," she said. "But I'd love it if you'd follow me back to Fox Hollow. I really do have to tell you something that can't wait until tomorrow."

Darren's pulse skipped and hopped, and he swallowed against it. "Is it bad?" Had she been leading him on tonight? Why had she agreed to go out with him if she was going to break up with him before the night ended?

He hated that his mind went to the fact that he deserved that. He didn't think Sarena was a mean person, and he shook his head. "Never mind. I'll take you to get your truck, and I'll follow you to Fox Hollow."

He did just that, parking behind her in front of the sprawling house at the end of a long lane off the highway. "Am I going to meet your sisters tonight?" he asked as he got out of his truck and approached her.

"No," she said with a laugh. She gathered her purse and turned toward him, slamming her door. "Give me a few minutes to go talk to them, and I'll meet you by the hammock on the west side of the garage." She beamed up at him, and Darren thought he'd meet her anywhere she said when she looked at him like that.

He could only nod, and he watched her hurry toward the front steps, noticing the limp in her left stride. He wondered if her foot hurt again, but he ducked his head and went toward the garage on the west end of the house.

The yard extended toward a stand of trees, and there he found the hammock Sarena mentioned. There was only one, and Darren let his fantasies run a little wild as he walked over to it and sat in it.

He hadn't looked at the clock in his truck or his phone when he'd arrived, and he laid down to wait. And wait. And wait.

Certainly more than ten minutes had passed, and Darren wondered what he should do. Wait? Text? Go home?

He decided to wait, hoping he wouldn't end up the fool sitting in the hammock all night long.

CHAPTER 4

"I have to tell him," Sarena said. "And I told him ten minutes, and it's been twenty at least." She shook her head as Sorrell started to say something else.

"I'm going. He's waiting, and if I don't tell him tonight, when should I do it?" She held up her hand, because she didn't want her sisters to answer that question. When she'd burst into the house with, "You'll never guess who I went to dinner with tonight," she'd expected some excitement.

They only had eighty-two days before one of them had to be married. She had to tell Darren about the stipulation in her father's will tonight. He might need some time to come to terms with what she was about to ask him to do.

"I'm going," she said. "I'll be back in a little bit."

"I'll put on the coffee," Serendipity said. "Strong coffee."

"I'll start the almond brittle," Sorrell said, though she didn't sound happy about it.

Sarena grabbed a couple of bottles of water and headed

out the back door, steeling herself for what she had to say within the next thirty minutes. The sun had gone down; the earth had started to cool. She wanted to take off her boots and socks and relax, but she had one more thing to do tonight.

She approached the hammock, and Darren started to sit up. "Don't get up," she said, extending a bottle of water toward him. "Sorry, that took longer than I thought it would."

"Yeah, I wasn't sure what I should do," he said. He took the bottle and opened it.

"My sisters are a little much to handle." She perched on the edge of the hammock, easily sliding back into Darren. She giggled as he lifted his arm and she settled against his chest.

She quieted and looked up into the sky, hardly able to see through the leaves to the stars beyond. "I love this spot," she said. "You know, after you called the paramedics and everyone came and took my father, this is where I came."

His fingers moved up and down on her arm, sending a shiver through her skin and muscles. "You knew I called the paramedics?"

"Yeah," she said. "It was a guess, because I hadn't, and neither had Sorrell or Serendipity. You were the only other person any of us had interacted with."

Darren hummed in the back of his throat, and Sarena tried really hard to find the right words.

"When I was a little boy," he said, his voice soft as silk and just as rich too. "My siblings and I would lie in the backyard like this, looking up at the sky and naming all the constellations we could. My father used to give whoever could spot the little dipper first an extra dollar on our allowance." He sounded full of joy as he spoke of the memory, and it made Sarena smile.

"How many brothers do you have?" she asked.

"Two," he said. "Both older than me."

"Sisters?"

"I've got two of them too," he said. "One younger than me, and one older."

"So you're fourth?"

"Yep." His hand tightened on her upper arm. "I'm slowly going mad here," he said. "Are you going to tell me whatever it is you need to tell me?"

"Yes." She cleared her throat. "Yes, I am." She drew in a deep breath, her mind completely blank. "Okay."

"Maybe just start at the beginning," he suggested.

"My dad died," Sarena said, and that unblocked everything. "And he had a will, right? Of course he did, because everyone who dies has a will—at least you do when you're his age. Anyway." She uncapped her bottle of water but didn't take a drink, because she didn't want to dump it all over her.

"Anyway," she said again. "We found out that in his will, he'd put that one of us girls has to be married—" Her voice stuck on the word, but she forced herself to keep going. "—in order to keep the ranch, or else it'll go to my uncle Dale. And let me tell you, that is *not* happening."

Fierce determination filled her, and her heartbeat calmed slightly.

Darren didn't move. He didn't breathe. He didn't speak.

"So there it is," she said. "I have to be married by Christmas—by December twenty-third if we're going to be

technical—and I was kind of hoping you'd be up for the job."
She twisted to look at him, hoping to get an idea of what he
thought of the idea, but the hammock made it hard for her to
get a good view. She only seemed to smash further into his
side.

"Married?" he finally said, the word more of a gasp than
anything else.

"It wouldn't be real," she said, quickly now, remembering
what Sorrell had advised her to say. "We just have to have the
paper. Then I'll get the ranch, and the stipulation will be met,
and everything will be great."

"But—but you'll be married," he said. "To me?"

"Just for a few months," she said. "At most." She pushed
against his chest and sat up, swinging her legs over the side of
the hammock and twisting to look back at him. There wasn't
much light back here, under the trees, and she couldn't get a
read on him.

He stared straight up, his eyes wide.

Sarena stood up, stepped away from the hammock, and
took a long drink of her water. Darren bolted to his feet a
moment later, and said, "I have to go."

"Darren," she said as he strode past her.

He paused but kept his back to her. He finally ducked his
chin, the side profile of his face illuminated by the lights on the
garage a few feet in front of him. "I'll call you tomorrow,
okay?"

"Okay," she said, nowhere near loud enough for him to
hear.

He left anyway, the roar of his truck engine starting

making Sarena wince. She sighed as he took off down the lane, and she couldn't go back in the house and face her sisters.

She tipped her head back and looked up into the night sky. Without as many branches and leaves above her, she could see a long strip of black sky. "Lord," she whispered. "Help us. I've worked so hard around this ranch, and I can't stand to lose it."

"Sarena?"

She turned toward the back corner of the house, where Sorrell stood. "I'm coming."

"Did he leave?"

"Yes," Sarena said miserably. She moved toward Sorrell, opening her arms for a hug as hot tears came to her eyes.

"Did you tell him?" Sorrell accepted her hug and held her tight.

"Yes," Sarena said. "I told him, and I'm pretty sure it freaked him out, and he left." She couldn't believe a fake marriage for a few months was worse that a false foot. "I didn't even get to tell him that we wouldn't have to live together or anything. Literally nothing would have to change."

"Maybe you should text him that," Sorrell said.

Sarena stepped back, a new light of hope in her chest. "You're right. I'm going to text him that right now." She started tapping, telling him he wouldn't have to move out of his cabin at Chestnut Ranch. They could still meet at the back fence.

Nothing would have to change, she finally added before sending the text.

"Come on," Sorrell said. "We're dying to hear about the date."

* * *

THE NEXT MORNING, Sarena woke with a bad taste in her mouth, like she'd forgotten to brush her teeth before bed. She hadn't, though, because she carried out a routine as if her life depended on it, and she'd definitely brushed her teeth.

She dragged herself into the bathroom and repeated the job, the peppermint waking her up slightly. Her throat hurt, because she'd stayed up too late talking with her sisters. Once Darren called, all the jitteriness in her stomach would settle down.

Of course he wouldn't call before breakfast, and Sarena didn't eat breakfast anyway, especially not after she'd gone to dinner with a man and eaten so much the night before. She felt like her stomach hadn't digested anything she'd eaten last night, and her limbs weighed her down as she went outside to get started on her chores.

She put the horses out in the pasture and worked in their stalls, cleaning them out and putting fresh sawdust in, as the forecast called for rain overnight. If she got the sawdust done now, she wouldn't have to work in the rain, and the horses would stay dry. She fed and watered the chickens and ducks, and then moved over to the maternity herd.

Sarena needed a good calving season in order to keep things going on the ranch, and she'd had an amazing breeding season. Her first calves should be delivered the first week of December, and she'd already hired two temporary cowboys who would be arriving the day after Thanksgiving. Jay and Hopper came every year, and she contracted them before they left Fox Hollow every March. They knew how she worked, and how her cattle acted, and Sarena didn't have to explain anything to them.

In addition to them, Sarena employed two full-time cowboys around the ranch, and she nodded to Theo as she saw him heading out into the fields. He'd drive the four-wheeler out through the whole herd to check on the to-be-mothers, because he knew as well as her that any cow that wasn't standing was in trouble.

Cows should be standing, and Sarena saw happy cows as far as she could see. She moved her attention to some book-keeping, which she did in an office in the homestead. Serendipity and Sorrell both worked in town, and Sarena loved the quiet solitude of the house when she existed there alone.

Sometimes she liked to play music while she calculated costs and budgets, and sometimes she really thrived in the quiet peace inside these walls. Today was one of those days, where she just wanted the silence to soar through her soul. It allowed her mind to focus on what she needed to do and think about.

Her paperwork seemed to take forever, because she kept getting distracted by thoughts of Darren. He hadn't called yet, and lunchtime was upon her. She finished writing the checks she needed to keep the electricity on for another month and keep her cowboys with her for another month, and she went into the kitchen to make lunch.

Sarena couldn't stomach much more than lettuce, so she made herself a salad and pulled out some lunchmeat to get some protein too. She'd skipped meals before and then tried to work the ranch in the afternoon, and that had never gone well. So she knew better than to pretend like she could eat a few bites of lettuce and tomato and call it good.

After lunch, she took a walk to the back fence, the note she'd written for Darren heavy in her pocket. She pinned it to the top rung on the fence, something she'd done in the past. Darren had never gotten any of those notes, though, and Sarena took a few minutes to look across the fence to Chestnut Ranch, wishing Darren would come driving up.

He didn't. Her phone stayed quiet. Eventually, she went back to the main ranch and completed the rest of the day's chores. The scent of garlic and onion met her nose before she entered the house, and she hoped Sorrell would have dinner almost done.

"Ten minutes," her sister said when Sarena walked in.

"Perfect," she said, stepping over to the sink to wash all the way to her elbows.

"Did he call?" Sorrell asked.

Sarena shook her head and focused on the apple-scented soap in front of her.

"He'll call." Sorrell returned to the stove as a timer went off, picked up the pot, and drained the potatoes in the sink next to her.

He didn't call while they ate dinner, and he didn't call even when Serendipity asked what in the world he was waiting for.

Darkness fell, and Sarena couldn't stand to stay in the house for another minute. She took her phone out to the front porch and restarted it, sure it hadn't had a proper signal all day. Otherwise, she'd have gotten Darren's phone call.

He'd said he'd call, and a special kind of desperation coated her stomach while she waited for her phone to restart.

It did, singing out the chime it did when it came back to life. She gave it several more seconds to connect to the Wi-Fi on the ranch, and she checked her voicemail first. No messages.

No missed calls.

He simply hadn't called.

Defeated, she sagged against the porch column, wondering what she should do now.

CHAPTER 5

Darren had not slept well after dropping Sarena off at her ranch. He wasn't even sure he'd fallen all the way into unconsciousness at all. When the first gray light had come through his window, he'd gotten up and taken Koda out.

The dog would run with him all day, but he threw a ball for the retriever, as he was still learning to fetch and bring the ball back. Actually, Koda needed to learn to drop the ball when Darren told him to, and he took out bits of hot dog with him to encourage the pup.

Once that was done, he made plenty of eggs for breakfast, because Koda liked them as much as Darren did. He thought about Sarena as he put hay in the loft. As he went out to the dog enclosure and fed, watered, and released the hounds.

Seth normally took care of all the dogs, but his operation had grown astronomically in the past year, and Darren helped every day, as did Russ or Rex.

He worked on a whole bunch of other stuff he couldn't even remember, because all he could think about was what Sarena had said. There was no way on this planet he could marry her, despite the texts she'd sent further explaining that nothing would have to change between them.

But Darren knew that something would change. He might not have to move in with her, but *everything* would change between them. He'd been married before; she hadn't. He knew things would change, and he honestly wasn't sure he could handle it.

Russ invited him to dinner at the homestead, and Darren went. He stayed longer than normal, because he couldn't get himself to leave. Because once he left, he'd have no reason not to call Sarena.

And yet, he couldn't call her.

"Come on," he said to his golden retriever. "Let's go for a ride."

Koda went to the door and put his nose on it, then jumped back when Darren turned the knob. He jumped up into the back of the truck, and Darren got behind the wheel. He seemed to know the way to Fox Hollow, and before he knew it, he was rumbling down the dirt road to the homestead where he'd held Sarena in the hammock last night.

He had no idea what he was going to say to her, but he couldn't just not call her when he'd said he would. The headlights flashed across the porch, and he saw Sarena standing there. His heart tumbled down to his boots as he realized his time to come up with something to say had dwindled to nothing.

He couldn't just sit in the truck, so he got out and looked at Koda. "Stay there, bud," he said almost under his breath. Then he faced the porch, tucking his hands in his pockets as he took slow steps toward Sarena, who'd come out from behind the column where she'd been standing.

"Hey," he said when he reached the bottom of the steps. He looked up at her, and she cocked her hip and folded her arms. "I have no idea what to say to you."

"You said you'd call."

"I couldn't," he said. "So I just came over." He took the five steps to the porch, and Sarena didn't give him even an inch. He took her into his arms, finally settling now that he could feel the warmth of her skin and breathe in the strawberry scent of her hair.

He took a long breath, glad when she inhaled with him.

"I can't lose the ranch," she said against his chest, and Darren's whole world narrowed to just the two of them, standing on the porch in the Texas Hill Country wilds.

"I want to help you," he said, keeping his arms around her so she couldn't see his face. "But Sarena, I don't know if I can do it."

She nodded, trying to pull away from him.

"Wait," he said.

"Darren, that's just it," she said, finally getting away from him. "I can't wait. I have literally eighty days."

"What about your sisters?"

She shook her head. "It's me, Darren. It's up to me." She reached up and wiped her eyes, though he hadn't seen any tears. "Thanks for coming over." She turned to go back inside, but Darren couldn't stand the sight of her walking away from him.

He darted around her, blocking her entrance back inside. "Wait."

"For what?" she demanded. "If you can't do it, you can't do it. I understand."

Darren's frustration built inside him and shot to the top of his head. He kept his head down as the words poured from his mouth. "I don't want to lose you."

She simply looked at him, and Darren knew he'd spoken true. "If it's lose you or marry you, I'll marry you." He couldn't believe what he'd just said, but the words had come out. He hadn't choked on them or stuttered over them. "Will you kiss me now, please? I don't want our next kiss to be at our wedding." He finally managed to put a grin on his face, but Sarena kept staring at him as if he'd spoken another language.

He chuckled, glad when she finally moved her hands up his arms to his shoulders. She made him feel strong, like she needed him to hold her up, when really, he needed her. He leaned down and she tipped her head up, and Darren kissed her.

Kissing her was like coming home. He'd always liked kissing Sarena, and this time was absolutely no different. He pushed his hands into her hair, hoping he hadn't just made the biggest mistake of his life.

He absolutely wanted her in his life; he just hadn't been prepared to make things so serious and so permanent quite so soon. He pulled away, and they breathed in together.

"I promise this will be easy for you," she whispered. "It'll be a simple ceremony. No one will know but us and my sisters. And well, our lawyer. And that's it."

Nothing about what she'd asked him to do would be easy for him. And yet, Darren wanted to do it. He wanted her to keep her ranch, because he'd seen her working on it, and he knew how very important to her it was.

"Thank you, Darren," she whispered, and he sure did like the sound of his name in her sultry voice.

"So what happens next?" he asked, thoughts of buying a diamond ring and getting down on one knee dancing through his head.

"Let me talk to my sisters. They're really the only ones that need to be there." She pulled away from him. "Unless you want to invite someone."

He thought for a moment, quickly bypassing any of the Johnson brothers, even Griffin. "No, I think I'm good." He'd invite them to his real wedding, but not a fake one. Then he'd have to make something up, and Darren wanted to lie as little as possible, especially to his bosses and friends—and himself.

"So I need to get a dress," she said, exhaling shakily. "And do you need to get a suit or something?"

"I wear stuff like that to church," he said, glad he'd started going again.

She nodded, her eyes wide and frightened. He wasn't sure why she wore such a look. She'd never been married before. Her spouse hadn't died. They weren't going to live together... were they?

She'd said they weren't, and Darren believed her. He put the thought out of his mind and looked at her.

"You want to introduce me to your sisters?" he asked, hooking his thumb over his shoulder. "I mean, I know I'm not going to live here." He watched her closely, and she didn't look like he'd said anything that wasn't true. "So maybe I should. Just so they know who I am should your uncle come around asking questions."

Sarena nodded. "They should at least be able to point you out, I suppose."

Darren reached behind him and scrambled his fingers along the wooden door until they met the knob. He twisted it, took her hand, and turned to go into the house. He'd never been inside here, as this was only his second visit to Fox Hollow Ranch.

"Nice place," he said, taking in the wide entry way that narrowed into a hallway that led back into the house. He peeked into the room to his right, but it was too dark to see much.

"Sorrell does all the decorating," Sarena said, squeezing his hand. "They're probably still watching TV." She led him down the hallway, and the house opened up into a giant room, half of which the kitchen took up, and the other half dominated by the living room.

Sure enough, two more women lounged on the couch, both of them with their feet up on an ottoman in front of them. They both had Sarena's dark hair and slim figures, and he wondered why one of them couldn't get married.

"Guys," Sarena said, and Darren felt her nerves pinching in his bloodstream. "Can we turn that off for a second? I want you to meet Darren."

"Oh, dear Lord in heaven," one of them said, jumping to her feet and reaching for the remote control in the next second. The TV went dark and mute, and Darren stood there facing Sarena's sisters.

He lifted his free hand in a half-hearted wave. "Hey."

"This is Darren Dumond," Sarena said. "And he's agreed to marry me."

One sister sucked in a breath as her eyes widened. The other shrieked, immediately covering her mouth with both hands. Darren just stood there, like a freak museum display they couldn't look away from.

"We thought you should meet him, so if Uncle Dale asks any questions, you can say of course you've met him, and he's been around here, and all of that." Sarena looked from them to him. "Darren, these are my sisters, Sorrell and Serendipity. They go in that order."

The shrieking sister came forward and drew him into a hug. "Thank you, Darren."

He really didn't need their gratitude, but he patted her awkwardly on the back. He looked at Sarena, and the question must've ridden in his eyes, because she said, "That's Sorrell. You might have seen her at the community center maybe. She's the director there for the city."

"Sure, okay," Darren said, though he'd only seen Sorrell at Griffin's wedding.

"And Serendipity." Sarena reached for her other sister, and she came skipping over. "She's a nature guide."

"Seems about right," Darren said, smiling at her. "And

unusual names you guys have." He looked around at the three sisters. "Is there a story there?"

"Our mother was a bit eccentric," Sarena said. "Her name was Susan, and she hated how plain it was. So she decided we had to have non-plain names. All with the letter S." She gave a sexy half-shrug and nudged Serendipity. "Stop staring at him."

"Sorry." Serendipity's smile didn't slip though. "He's handsome, Sarena. You didn't say that."

"Yes, she did," Sorrell said, returning to the end table to pick up her empty glass. "Lots of times." She gave Sarena a knowing look and Darren a sly smile before continuing past him and into the kitchen.

He suddenly had the very real urge to get on home. Surely they'd both seen him before. They'd sat by him at the wedding, at least for a few minutes.

"Well, I left my dog in the back of my truck, and a cowboy gets up real early these days." He reached up to tip his hat to the Adams sisters. "It was a real pleasure meetin' y'all."

He cursed himself for turning into some cowboy hick, and when he looked at Sarena, he knew she'd heard it. He leaned down as if he'd kiss her right in front of her sisters, thought better of it, and strode toward the hallway that led to freedom.

Sarena caught him at the front door, sliding one hand up his chest. "*I'll* call *you* tomorrow, okay?"

He shook his head, because when it was just the two of them, things were easier. He could talk to Sarena, even if she had told her sisters how handsome he was. If he had brothers or friends, he'd tell them how beautiful she was.

You have friends. And brothers, he told himself. And he

did. But he had not mentioned the idea of a fake marriage to any of them. He couldn't believe he'd even considered it for more than five seconds, let alone agreed to it.

He'd gone mad. That was the only explanation.

"No, I can't call you?"

"No," he said. "I'll pick you up for dinner at six-thirty? Does that work?"

A smile stretched across that mouth he liked so much. "Sure, that works."

"Great," he said. "Let's try to plan this wedding quickly."

She tipped up and kissed him, and everything male in Darren wanted to make sure Sarena got her happy ending. Whatever that looked like for her, he wanted her to have it. He knew what unhappy endings looked like, and felt like, and tasted like, and he did not wish that on anyone.

"Tomorrow," she said, her lips catching against his. He nodded, opened the door, and went on home with Koda.

Engaged, sang through his mind as he lay in bed thirty minutes later. The thought wasn't entirely terrible, but Darren still couldn't smile as he lay in bed, unable to sleep. He never thought he'd be engaged again, and something dangerous and poisonous rolled through his stomach.

It's not real, he told himself. *It's not, Diana.*

And somehow, that made things a little better, though he knew it was dangerous to play with serious things. Not only that, but what he'd said earlier about not wanting to lose Sarena was very, very real—and he couldn't explain that to Diana.

Or himself.

CHAPTER 6

Sarena stood back and smoothed the front of the dress down before looking up into the mirror. Buying a dress for a fake wedding seemed like a complete waste of money. What in the world was she doing here?

"I like that one," Sorrell said from her spot in the wing-back chair. It was covered with red velvet, and Sorrell perched on it like she was a queen.

Sarena had refused to go to the only bridal shop in Chestnut Springs. If she did that, not only would her shopping trip become headline news, but there'd be a whole article about how the reclusive daughter had finally left the ranch.

She'd left the ranch a couple of nights ago too, she wanted people to know. But not really.

She didn't honestly care what people thought about her. Surely someone had seen her at dinner with Darren a few nights ago, and if they saw her then modeling wedding dresses...

Sarena wanted to avoid that as much as possible. So Serendipity had looked up the next-closest bridal shop, and they'd driven an hour to Temple. It was a bigger city anyway, and hey, they had red velvet chairs for her sisters to sit in.

"Yeah?" Sarena asked. "I think it pulls funny under my arms." Probably because her bust was a little too busty.

"We can take that out," the woman helping them said. Gail smiled at her and yanked on the fabric under Sarena's arm. "Easily. Give you a little more room there. Would that work?"

Anything would work for a fake marriage. Sarena kept the words in her mind, though, because this had to look real. Once Uncle Dale found out about the marriage, Sarena expected to have to field a lot of questions from her family. But for right now, no one needed to know. She hadn't invited Aunt Scottie, or any of the cousins in town. She'd literally texted Darren last night after he'd dropped her off after their date and asked, *How about next Saturday?*

Great, he'd said.

Great, as if marrying her would really be great. She knew Darren liked her. She could see it every time he looked at her. She felt it in the way he touched her, and the way he kissed her. He'd said right out loud he couldn't lose her.

A tiny part of Sarena wanted the wedding to be real. Every day, that part grew a little bit, and Sarena had to lie down every night and tell herself not to get carried away. She and Darren would *not* be getting married right now if she didn't have a deadline. But still, as she slept, her mind seemed to be working out a way for the marriage to *become* real.

Maybe over time... she kept thinking.

And so she'd wanted a real wedding dress. Sorrell had ordered a fancy cake from the bakery in town, being sure not to make it look too much like a wedding cake. It also wasn't just one out of the case either.

Her sisters had gotten new dresses, and they'd been working on the back deck since Sarena had come inside and introduced them to Darren.

"Try on the last one," Serendipity said. "Then you'll know which one to get."

Gail had chosen three dresses for Sarena, and the first had been hideous. Too much lace, and not enough fabric across that busty bust of hers. But this dress...would do.

Sarena wanted a dress that did better than that. So she went back into the massive dressing room and let Gail unzip her out of one dress and button her into another.

Gail smiled like she'd just won a million bucks as she gathered the fabric of the gown and followed Sarena out of the room.

"Oh, my." Sorrell actually stood up, the phone she usually swiped around on forgotten. "Sarena." She looked up from the yards of fabric and met Sarena's eyes. She actually started crying, and Sarena's pulse pounced through her whole body.

"Are those good tears?"

"Turn and look," Gail said as Serendipity stood too.

Sarena did as Gail said, the image of the woman in the mirror someone completely foreign to her eyes. This dress was almost the color of almond milk—not quite white, and definitely not tan either. It shone with a glimmer Sarena couldn't explain, and the sleeve circled her biceps and left her shoulders bare.

There was enough fabric to contain her bust and allow her arms to move, something Sarena had thought she'd have to compromise on. The torso lay flat and tight against her skin, and then the full skirt billowed out and down, covering her feet.

That was an absolute must. Sarena couldn't wear high heels, and she didn't want to get married in work boots. She'd thought the best thing to do would be to go barefoot, and that meant the dress had to cover her feet completely.

Not that anyone would be there to see them.

Didn't matter; it was her wedding, and that tiny part of her that wanted it to be real wanted to make sure her feet were covered. Then she'd be as comfortable as she could be at her own fake wedding.

"Oh," she said softly as Sorrell came to her right side and Serendipity came to her left. They hugged her arms, their smiles made of magic.

"This is the one," Sorrell said, and she swiped at her eyes. "You're so beautiful."

"Thank you for doing this for us," Serendipity said, and Sarena's eyes flew to hers in the mirror. Thankfully, Gail stood back, letting the sisters have their private moment right there in the middle of the bridal shop, and she didn't hear Serendipity.

Sarena just nodded, and her sisters retreated to their red velvet chairs. "This is the one I want," she said, but she didn't move to go take it off so they could purchase it and go.

She had plenty to do around the ranch that day. Always more to do. But she stood there and stared at herself, the vision of the perfect bride—something she'd actually thought she'd never be.

Something she'd thought she never even wanted.

She hadn't known how much a man could add to her life until she'd met Darren Dumond, and she couldn't believe God had somehow convinced him that marrying her was a good idea.

She tore her eyes away from herself, more determined than ever to make sure this fake marriage did not make his life harder in any way. "Yep," she said, striding back to the dressing room. "This is the one I want."

* * *

Several hundred dollars lighter, Sarena returned to the ranch with her sisters. She'd have to take the morning on Thursday to go back to Temple to pick up the dress, which needed some minor alterations done.

"Cake and dress and venue," she said as she followed Sorrell and Seren into the farmhouse. "What else?"

"Dinner?" Sorrell asked. "Will he stay for a dinner with us?"

"I'll talk to him," she said.

"We could invite Theo and Phillip," Seren said. "Make it a ranch thing."

"I can't wear my wedding dress if we do that," Sarena said, shaking her head. "No, I'm going to give them the whole weekend off. Tell them to go visit their folks or whatever. I don't even want them here while Darren is here."

"They should probably see him around." Seren said as she set a bag of doughnuts on the kitchen counter. "That'll make your relationship more plausible."

"The relationship is plausible," Sarena said, maybe with slightly too much sass. Seren looked at her, her dark eyes widening in surprise.

"Sorry," Sarena said. "I just..." She didn't want to tell her sisters she actually really liked Darren. So much. She wasn't going to let that little part of herself come out verbally. It would be too painful once the marriage had to end.

She could barely swallow as it was, and the nuptials hadn't even been said yet.

"You're just stressed," Sorrell said. "We all are." She opened the box of chocolates she'd bought at a specialty shop in Temple. "Let's have chocolate and make a menu for the wedding dinner."

Sarena let Sorrell ply her with chocolate as she simply nodded to whatever Sorrell wanted to put on the wedding menu. She didn't care, and she didn't think Darren would.

She had to first tell him about the dinner anyway.

She plowed through the next several days, letting Serendipity do different hairstyles at night, driving to Temple to get the dress, and sampling the hot artichoke dip Sorrell made as part of the appetizer plate for the wedding.

Before she knew it, Saturday arrived, and with it, so did Darren. His blue and white truck pulled up to the farmhouse around ten, and Sarena sat on the front porch, waiting for him in a pair of jeans and a white T-shirt with a blue heart on the front.

"You came," she said, a touch of surprise in her voice.

Darren glanced at her as he let his dog out of the back of the truck. Koda galloped toward Sarena, who laughed. "Oh, look at you," she said, scrubbing him down as he wound around her legs. "You're getting so big. Look at your paws. You're huge." She giggled and smiled at the cute little puppy, and then switched her gaze to Darren. "He's going to be huge."

"Sixty or seventy pounds," Darren agreed. He wore a smile, a pair of jeans, and a leather jacket over a gray T-shirt. He carried a garment bag in one hand and a hat box in the other, and Sarena couldn't wait to see him all dressed up.

He'd invited her to church last weekend, but Sarena hadn't been able to get herself off the ranch in time for the services. With all the wedding prep, she was behind in every aspect of the ranch, and she and Darren had only been out once that week.

He'd parked that truck in front of the farmhouse a couple of times, and they'd gone out to get her chores done together. She'd loved spending time with him on her land, and Theo and Phillip had both met Darren. So her marriage to him, should it ever become public, wouldn't come out of thin air.

Her lungs vibrated, something they'd been doing for seven days now whenever she thought too long about what her life would be like after October tenth.

After her wedding day.

It's going to be exactly the same, she told herself.

"The wedding is still at eleven, right?" Darren asked.

"Yes," Sarena said, turning to go back up the steps. "Come on in. You can get ready in the spare bedroom."

She'd get ready in her bedroom, with both of her sisters, just the way she'd always imagined. So there were some parts of this wedding that were exactly how Sarena wanted them.

Darren disappeared into the bedroom, and Sarena went further down the hall to hers. Sighing, she closed the door just as Sorrell came out of the attached bathroom.

"There you are," her sister said. "We have less than an hour."

"He's here," Sarena said, and she wished she didn't sound so miserable about it. She should be happy, as she'd get to marry the handsome, kind, smart, hardworking Darren Dumond.

She stepped into her dress, and Serendipity buttoned the back of it. She took Sarena into the bathroom, where she sat on a padded stool so Seren could do her hair. Sorrell painted her face up just right, and within forty-five minutes, Sarena was ready to walk down the aisle.

The three of them were going to walk toward Darren together, and the only other person who would be there was Janelle Stokes, who had the power in the good state of Texas to make a marriage legal and binding.

The doorbell rang, and Sorrell dropped the makeup brush she'd been putting back in the bag. "That'll be Janelle. I'll get it." She hurried out of the bathroom, and Seren met Sarena's eyes in the mirror.

"This is going to be fine," Seren said. "You like him, and he likes you, and you never know...maybe the two of you can make a real marriage out of this." She hugged Sarena's shoulders and smiled.

"No," Sarena said after a moment, because she didn't want Seren to think she'd been hoping for that exact thing. She thought of the anguish on Darren's face when he'd told her about his first wife. "I don't think that will happen."

She stood slowly and gave herself a few seconds to find and keep her balance. "But we'll get to keep the ranch, and that's what's important."

Her heart didn't matter, and though it increased its rate as she went down the hall and out to the kitchen, she kept dismissing the fact that her most important organ was about to break.

"Are you ready?" Janelle asked, and Sarena wanted to grab onto her and hold her tight. Find some sort of steady, stable ground to stand on. Instead, she just nodded.

"Darren's out there, and you're all ready, so let's just start, shall we?" Janelle put a huge smile on her face, as if she was just so happy to be sharing in Sarena's special day.

"Okay," Sarena said.

Janelle put both hands on Sarena's shoulders and leaned down, her bright blue eyes earnest and sparkling. "Put on a smile, Sarena. You like this man, right? And he likes you enough to do this, and no one's getting duped here."

Sarena nodded, turned away from Janelle for a moment, and practiced her happy-bride smile. It almost sat right on her face, and when she faced the back of the house again, she kept the smile precisely where it should be.

"All right," she said. "I'm ready." She linked arms with Serendipity on her left and Sorrell on her right, and they walked to the door Janelle had left open.

She stood at the far end of the deck with Darren, and they both faced Sarena and her sisters as they stepped outside.

Sarena focused on Darren, and the lane between them narrowed. He'd always called to her very core, and today was no different.

He looked downright mouthwatering in a dark gray suit, with a white shirt underneath the jacket, and a blue, gray, and green tie knotted at his neck. His cowboy hat matched the suit, and she'd never seen it before. She knew it wasn't the same one he sweated through while he worked around Chestnut Ranch, and her gratitude almost made her next step into a stumble.

Sorrell's grip on her elbow increased, and Sarena reminded herself how much she loved her sisters and her ranch.

She made it all the way to Darren, who leaned down and pressed his lips to her cheek. He whispered, "You are absolutely gorgeous," before he turned toward Janelle.

"Are you two ready for this?" she asked, that bright smile still in place.

Darren looked at Sarena, and Sarena looked at Darren.

"Ready," they said together.

CHAPTER 7

Darren couldn't believe what he was doing. It almost felt like he'd left his body at some point, and he flew above the scene on the back deck at Sarena's farmhouse. He could hear Janelle speaking, and talking about what it took to make a marriage work. Love, compassion, sacrifice, compromise.

Darren agreed with all of that. For sure. He'd been married before, and he knew he didn't get to leave his dirty socks under the bed or that there wasn't a maid to come behind him and clean up his breakfast dishes.

He really thought he'd learned those things *after* Diana had died, though, when she suddenly wasn't there to lovingly put his dirty plate in the dishwasher. It had still been there when he'd gotten home from working the ranch she'd loved, and he'd had to load it into the rack himself.

He watched as he glanced at Sarena, the feeling of...affection overcoming him. In that moment, he zoomed back into his body, almost as if he just now realized what was happening.

He was marrying this woman. And while he couldn't say he was thrilled about it, he wasn't super upset about it either. He didn't know what that meant, but he gripped her arm and kept her close.

Sarena Adams possessed a beauty unlike any Darren had ever seen before. And when she'd come walking toward him, Darren had felt...lucky.

She smelled like summer-ripened peaches and sunshine, and when Janelle asked him if he'd take her to be her lawfully wedded wife, Darren said, "I will."

Janelle Stokes pronounced them man and wife—he'd missed Sarena's pledge to him—and added, "You can kiss your bride." She smiled like this was a real wedding, with two people who really loved each other.

Darren turned woodenly to Sarena, a hint of embarrassment creeping through his veins. He hadn't kissed a woman in front of someone for a very long time, and her sisters were watching too.

But he bent down, noticing her smile just before his mouth touched hers. The inferno that raged through him every time he kissed Sarena burst to life, and Darren worked to tame it. The last thing he needed was to make out with her as if he couldn't control himself.

You're not her husband, no matter what a piece of paper says, he told himself. Pulling away, he wiped his mouth to make sure he didn't wear her lipstick in the pictures.

Pictures. He almost groaned out loud. The last thing he

needed was digital evidence of what they'd done that morning. But Sarena needed it, in case her uncle came claiming she hadn't gotten married.

Darren turned toward Sorrell and Serendipity, realizing only Janelle was clapping from behind him. The other two Adams sisters gaped at him and Sarena, and he glanced at his new bride to try to figure out why.

"Congratulations, you two," Janelle said. She appeared in front of them, a piece of paper in her hand. "You take this to the courthouse, and they'll mail you your marriage certificate in a couple of weeks."

"Thank you," Sarena said, taking the paper. Darren was still trying to catch up to everything, and he felt completely out of breath.

Janelle turned to leave, and Sorrell asked her if she could stay. "I really can't," she said. "But thanks for inviting me." She went into the house, leaving Darren with the three Adams sisters.

"Okay," Serendipity said brightly. Too brightly. "We have lunch inside. Let's eat, shall we?"

Darren watched Sarena nod, and he put a bit of pressure on her arm to get her to stay with him while her sisters went ahead. "What's going on?" he asked.

"What do you mean?"

"I mean, they didn't applaud, didn't hug you, and they're staring at me like I grew another head during the ceremony." He tore his gaze from the back of Sorrell's head to look at Sarena. "You wanted this, right?"

"Of course," she said. "We *all* wanted this." She glanced at them too. "Honestly, I think they might be in shock."

Darren certainly was, but he didn't think that was it at all. Their eyes met again, and Darren pressed his cheek to Sarena's. He breathed, and it was so much easier with her so close to him. "Go to dinner with me tonight?" he asked.

"Yes," she whispered.

"Not that the wedding luncheon isn't going to be amazing," he said. "But we'll have to eat again later, won't we?"

"I will," Sarena said, still standing within the circle of his arms, right where he wanted her. "Because I've been too nervous to eat much the last few days."

"You have?" He pulled back and peered down at her. "Why's that?"

Something crossed her face, and Darren categorized it easily. She had a secret, and he suddenly burned to know what it was.

"Just nervous," she said, and she took a step backward.

Darren didn't want to let her get away with that; they should be honest with each other. They were married now. He also didn't want to learn something that could ruin this moment, so he let her retreat from him, only reaching for her hand as they crossed into the house together.

"There you are," Serendipity said as if she'd been looking all over for them for the past hour. "I wasn't sure if you were going to come in."

"We came in, Seren," Sarena said, and she waited for Darren to pull her chair out for her. She picked up most of her skirts and sat down, smoothing everything after she'd settled.

She really took his breath away, and it took Darren another moment to get himself to sit down beside her.

After that, her sisters brought more food to the table than the four of them could ever eat, and Darren marveled at what they'd done for this fake occasion.

The conversation during lunch was stilted at best, and Darren did his best to try to contribute. The fact was, he didn't feel like talking, and it seemed like no one else did either.

"I'm going to go change," Sarena said. "Then I have work to do on the ranch."

"I'll help." Darren wiped his mouth and tossed his napkin on his empty plate.

"Did you bring work clothes?" she asked.

"I can wear what I had on before," he said, following her down the hall. He paused at the closed door that led into the bedroom where he'd changed previously and watched Sarena glide all the way to the end of the hall. She too hesitated and looked back at him, and Darren's smile burst onto his face spontaneously.

Thankfully, Sarena smiled back, and then she went into her bedroom. Darren did the same, changing much faster than his new wife.

Out in the kitchen again, he helped Serendipity clean up, neither of them with much to say. He liked the spirit here at Fox Hollow, he knew that. These sisters loved each other, and it wasn't until he heard a sniffle that he realized Sorrell had rejoined them.

He wanted to ask her if she was okay, but when Serendipity didn't, Darren kept his mouth shut too.

"I didn't actually know you liked my sister," Sorrell said, making Darren freeze to the spot.

"Sorrell," Serendipity warned. "Don't."

"What?" she asked. "Did you see the way he kissed her?" She looked from Serendipity to Darren, her eyes wide and bright. "You really like her."

She wasn't asking, and Darren wouldn't have denied it anyway. "Yes," he said.

"So maybe this could turn into something real," Sorrell said.

"Sorrell," Serendipity said again, her voice sharp this time. She jumped between Darren and Sorrell. "Don't listen to her, Darren. She has a very romantic imagination."

Darren turned away from both of them, taking the two plates he carried all the way to the sink. His thoughts ran away from him, though he tried to chase after them.

He'd be lying if he said he hadn't thought about what a real marriage with Sarena would be like. Of course he'd *thought* about it. Any man who kissed her would be thinking about it.

He knew very well that the only reason Sarena hadn't been married yet was because she didn't date. If she did, and she allowed anyone to kiss her, that man would've snapped her up and made her his. The first time Darren had kissed her, that was how he'd felt. He still did.

He'd just gotten scared. Too deep inside his mind, something he did from time to time.

"What's going on?" Sarena asked, thawing him from where he'd frozen in front of the sink. "What did you say to him?"

"Nothing," Sorrell said as Darren turned.

Sarena frowned at her sisters and looked at Darren. She wore a pair of blue jeans that seemed welded to her legs, the boots he'd seen countless times before, and a red and white checkered shirt. As she approached, he watched the concern roll across her face.

"What did they say?"

"Nothing," he said. "I think Sorrell was surprised to learn that I actually like you." He put a smile on his face. He wasn't saying anything she didn't already know. And he now knew why the pair of sisters had been staring at him so hard they'd forgotten to clap after the I-do.

He looked over Sarena's shoulder to the other two women, giving them a smile too.

Sarena turned back to them, her frustration like a scent on the air. "I told you guys I liked him."

"You should see the way he kisses you," Sorrell said. "That man *really* likes you."

Darren wouldn't deny that either, but he said nothing. Sarena turned and looked at him, and the questions in her eyes surprised him.

"She's not wrong," he said softly, sure the sisters couldn't hear. "Can I talk to you for a minute?" He took her hand in his and started for the back door. Sarena came with him, and he told himself to slow down so she wouldn't trip. He led her past where they'd been married, down the back steps, and over to the hammock they'd been lying in when she'd proposed this preposterous plan.

When he turned back to her, some of his emotions had settled. "Tell me you know I like you."

"Of course I know that."

"That I *really* like you." He tried to say it like her sister, but Darren didn't quite achieve it.

"I mean...I—I don't know."

"You don't know?" Darren didn't know how to make it more obvious.

"You broke up with me," she said. "We've only been back together for a week. I don't know." Her dark eyes flashed with danger, and Darren released a bit more of his irritation.

"I explained about why I broke up with you," he said. "Did you not hear me say I couldn't lose you? You think that comes from a place of mild attraction for a person?"

Sarena toed the ground with her right foot. "I've had a lot to deal with."

So had he, but he'd never actually thought Sarena didn't like him. He'd always known she did. She held his hand and kissed him. She went out with him when he asked. They talked and laughed and shared things with each other.

"Well," he said, reaching up and putting two fingers under her chin. He gently got her to look at him. "In case you're unclear, Sarena, I *really* like you." He leaned down and kissed her, letting himself go a little further than he had before.

He'd never wanted to kiss another woman when he'd first experienced Sarena's lips against his, and that feeling was only solidified with this kiss.

Her fingers slid up the side of his face and into his hair, dislodging his cowboy hat. He didn't care, though he took great pride in his hats and always hung them carefully so Koda wouldn't get one and chew it.

He relished the feeling of this woman's skin against his, and he only pulled away because Koda started barking.

Drawing in a deep breath, Darren looked over his shoulder toward the front of the farmhouse, where he'd parked his truck. Another dog started barking, and then another.

"Someone's here," Sarena said, her voice more of a scared whisper.

"Is that bad?" he asked, holding her tight.

"Depends on who it is," she said, stepping out of his embrace. He whistled for Koda to stop barking and come back to his side, which the dog did.

Sarena's ranch dogs kept barking, though, and her step slowed the closer to the road she got. Darren stayed right where he was, which was a good thing when Sarena spun back to him, her eyes wide with fear.

"Go," she said. "Hide."

"Hide?"

"It's my uncle," she said, taking a couple of short steps back toward him. "Go, Darren. Take Koda to the long horse barn to the west. Now."

"Okay," he said, reaching down and picking up his puppy. He watched Sarena turn back to the road and stride that way, purpose in her steps. The growl of a big engine reached his ears, and then Darren slipped into the trees and out of sight, feeling like a complete coward as he left his wife to deal with her uncle by herself.

CHAPTER 8

Sarena really did not possess the right type of kindness to deal with Uncle Dale. Why was he even here? Had he heard anything about the wedding?

Impossible, Sarena told herself. Literally five people knew about the wedding, and Sorrell and Serendipity would never say anything. Janelle wouldn't either, and Darren didn't even know her uncle's name.

"You don't need to get out," she called as the door opened on the driver's side. Curse her foot. Sarena couldn't move much faster than she already did, and her annoyance skyrocketed.

Thankfully, Uncle Dale did not get out. He had a bad back, something Sarena's father had told her about countless times. *He only wants the ranch so he can sell it*, her father's words echoed in her ears. *He has no family pride, and he hasn't worked in over twenty years.*

He would not be living it up for the next twenty years on the proceeds of this ranch, that was for dang sure.

Sarena reached the truck, and motioned for her uncle to roll down the window on the passenger side. He took his sweet time doing it, causing Sarena to growl in the back of her throat.

"What are you doing here, Uncle Dale?" she asked. Thank the heavens above that he hadn't shown up unexpectedly even thirty minutes ago. She'd have still been in her wedding dress, evidence of a big event on the dining room table.

"I came to see about the will," Uncle Dale said.

"I know all about the will," Sarena said, leaning into the truck to ease the pressure on her foot. "We've already talked about this."

"I wondered where you were on it," he said.

Sarena didn't know how to answer. She couldn't very well tell him that she'd gotten married that very morning. "It's none of your business," she said. "I don't have to answer to you."

"If you don't get married, this place is mine," he said.

"I understand the will," Sarena said. "And I have at least seventy more days, so you need to get off my ranch." She fell back a step, hoping he'd roll up the window and go.

He didn't. He didn't even close his door. "You're not selling all the equipment or anything, are you?" He narrowed his eyes at her. "Because that's not fair."

"Uncle Dale," she said. "What we do around this ranch is not your concern. It's none of your business."

"You can't just leave me with a ranch that has nothing," he said.

"Actually," she said. "I can. There's no stipulation in the will that says I can't burn the fields, knock down every building, and sell every animal before you take over. All it says is that I have to be married by December twenty-third." She stepped back into the truck, trying to tame her temper. She often said too much when her head got hot like this. "So I'll do what I want with the ranch while I own it. You'll *never* get it from me. Not if there's a single breath left in my body."

She pulled in a breath and reminded herself that she'd already won this battle. The whole war, too. She'd gotten married an hour ago.

"Sarena Adams," Uncle Dale said, and he sounded so much like her father that it sent a barb right through her chest. Her dad had chastised her like that when she gave him sass. "Don't talk to me like that."

"Get off my ranch," Sarena said, schooling her irritation behind a quiet voice.

"I'll see you in court," he said. "I'm going to file a motion that says you can't burn the fields and sell all the cattle."

"You do that," Sarena said, knowing she'd win. She'd already asked Janelle about it, and Janelle was the best family lawyer in ten counties.

Uncle Dale pulled his door closed with a slam, and put his truck in reverse. He dang near backed into the huge oak tree that lined the drive before he got the truck going the right way down the dirt lane that led to the highway.

Sarena unclenched her fingers, not even realizing she'd

been holding them so tightly, and watched until the red truck disappeared from view. She probably didn't need to send Darren scampering through the trees to the back barn, but she hadn't wanted Uncle Dale to see him. She should've known he wouldn't get out of his truck if he didn't have to. Sarena out-worked him ten to one, even with only one foot.

"Who was that?" Sorrell asked from the porch, and Sarena turned that way.

"No one," Sarena said, releasing the last of her adrenaline. "I'm going to get the chores done. Darren and I are going to dinner tonight."

Sorrell grinned from the porch, the perfect picture of beautiful farm girl. Well, farm girl with perfect fashion sense. That was Sorrell. She'd gotten all the fairer features from their mother, with the perfectly perky nose and delicate cheekbones. Sarena definitely had bigger bones and more meat on them too. But she'd never minded being Sorrell's older, uglier sister.

"I really think Seren is right," Sorrell said, and Sarena got moving. "He could be the one," she called after her.

Sarena didn't want to be rude to her sister, but she wasn't going to perpetuate this conversation. They didn't need to know that yes, she thought the same thing as them—that maybe Darren could be her real husband one day. Maybe they could fall in love for real, and make a real marriage out of their fake one.

She saw work to do everywhere she looked on the ranch, but she passed it all and went to the barn where she'd told

Darren to wait for her. Whether he'd found the right place or not, she wasn't sure.

She opened the door and peered inside. "Darren?"

"I'm in the loft," he said, the sounds of scuffling coming from overhead. He poked his head over the edge, and she smiled up at him. He really was the most wonderful man in the world, and Sarena couldn't believe she'd somehow caught his eye.

"Taking a nap?"

"I wish," he said, not returning the smile. "How did things go? Is he gone?"

Sarena nodded as she moved over to the ladder that led to the loft. She took the steps one at a time, making sure she had good balance on each one before lifting her foot to go to the next one. Darren put his hand in hers and pulled her up once she'd reached the top and didn't have anything to hold onto.

"Yeah," she said. "It went well enough. He left, and that's all I care about."

"What did he want?" Darren took her easily into his arms, and Sarena slipped her hands up his chest as if she'd done it countless times before. She hadn't, but she was comfortable with him. Completely comfortable.

"The same thing he's wanted every other time he's dropped by since Daddy died. He's fishing for information to find out what I'm doing with the ranch, or how close I am to getting married."

"Did you tell him we'd gotten married?"

"Nope."

"When are you going to tell him?"

"I'm not," Sarena said. "Nowhere in the will does it say I have to notify him when I get married. He can look it up through the court system, the same way anyone else can."

He gazed down at her, something storming in his eyes she didn't understand. She didn't want to deal with anything more today. At least not anything hard. "Can you just kiss me, please?" she asked, letting her smile come out.

A slow smile crossed his face too, and he dipped his head to kiss her. Warmth filled Sarena from top to bottom, and she sure did enjoy kissing her husband.

"Do we have to go do chores?" he whispered, pressing his cheek to hers as he started to sway with her.

"We do," she said. "But we can stay here a while longer if you want."

"I do," he said, taking her hand and pulling her over to a bed of straw.

"You made yourself a little bed, is that it?"

"That's it," he said, sitting down and laying back against a couple of bales. His dog moved for him, and then curled into his side. "You gotta move, bud." He pointed to his other side. "Sarena's gonna sit there."

The dog didn't move, and Darren picked him up and moved him, adoration in his eyes. He looked up at Sarena and offered her his hand. She took it and let him help her snuggle into his side. She sighed, all of the tension she'd been harboring in her body flowing out. "This is nice," she said. "I never take a day off."

"I understand the feeling," he said. "We really should take a day."

"I gave my cowboys the day off today." She sure did like the steady rhythm of his heart in her ear. "So we have to at least get around and feed and water the small animals."

"We will," he said. "I just want to lay here for a little bit." He exhaled, and Sarena liked how comfortable they were together. "Feels nice to just be together, doesn't it?"

"Yes," she murmured, letting her eyes drift closed. She'd never climbed up into the loft in the barn and snuck in a nap, but she thought she should start. *Only if Darren comes with you*, she thought, because she didn't think this rest period would be nearly as peaceful or nearly as fun without him.

Sometime later, an alarm on his phone rang, and she groaned with him. He silenced the alarm and shifted beside her. "Do we have to go?" she asked.

"Yeah," he said. "That's the rule of midday naps. When the alarm goes off, you get up and get back to work."

"You have a rule for midday naps," she said.

"Sweetheart, I have a rule for everything." Darren steadied her as she stood, and then he got to his feet. Their eyes met, and Sarena studied him, having just learned something new about him. "What?" he asked.

"You really have a rule for everything."

"Most things," he said. "It helps me get through the day."

"Is it hard for you to get through the day?"

Darren shrugged and ducked his head as he bent to pick up his cowboy hat. "Some days."

"Everyone has hard days," she said.

"Yep. And that's why I have some rules for myself. Otherwise, I'd lay in bed all day."

"Really?"

He paused getting himself put back together. "Sarena, my wife died. I felt like I lost everything that day. It's taken me a long time to recover. Some days, I still feel like it's the very next day after I buried her."

Sarena took a moment to absorb all that he'd said, because Darren didn't usually say so much at once. "I understand. I feel that way about my injury sometimes. Like, I wake up at home, and I hear a beep, and I'm a decade in the past, waking up in the hospital and learning I lost my foot."

"So you get it."

"I get it." She reached for his hand, pressing her palm against his. His hand dwarfed hers, but she loved the feel of her skin against his. "But I can't lay in bed all day, because there's a whole ranch to run."

"Lying in bed all day isn't that fun anyway," he said, another soft smile coming her way. He put his arm around her waist and pulled her into his body.

"You've done it?"

"Many times," he said. "It's not all it's cracked up to be. Although, I do have Koda now, and lying in bed with a dog might just be amazing."

Sarena laughed with him, the atmosphere between them so casual and carefree. They went down the ladder to the ground, and Sarena led him over to the goat pasture. They filled the water troughs and moved onto the chickens.

They fed and watered all living things on the ranch, and though Sarena got sweaty and then the dust stuck to that sweat, she loved the work. She liked looking over and seeing

Darren working those muscles as he lifted a bale of hay over a fence as if it weighed nothing. He checked with her before he did things, and that made her feel smart and powerful. His very presence made her feel like her life had new meaning, and she hadn't anticipated that.

By the time they'd finished, the sun hung in the west, and Sarena's stomach shrieked at her to eat something.

"Done?" Darren asked, taking off his gloves and clapping them together.

"Yes, sir," she said, wanting to skip over to him. But her skipping days had ended a long time ago.

He looked at her with an edge in his eyes, and Sarena wanted to know what it meant. So she asked, "Why are you looking at me like that?"

"Honestly?"

"We're married now," she said, the teasing spirit inside her drying up. "We should be as honest with each other as we can. Don't you think?"

"Yes," he said, his throat working as he swallowed. "We should." He tucked the gloves in his back pocket and adjusted his cowboy hat. With the trimmed beard and the deep, dark eyes, and the muscles, he called to everything female in Sarena.

"I'm looking at you like however I'm looking at you, because I think you're downright beautiful." He nodded, like that was that. Argument made.

Sarena blinked at him. "Wow."

"Wow?"

"You just said it out loud."

"You said we should be honest."

"I just...yeah." She took a couple of steps toward him, so much to tell him teeming just beyond her vocal cords. She couldn't tell him she wanted to try for a real marriage. He'd simply called her beautiful. That was a lot different than taking a fake marriage and making it real.

"So, honestly, Sarena," he said. "I really like you, as I've said before. I'm glad I could help you, and I still don't want to lose you."

"So...what does that mean? Where do you see this going? Is it going somewhere? Or is it just until my uncle backs off?"

Darren shrugged. "I don't have all those answers."

"None of them?"

"Do you?"

Sarena opened her mouth to answer him, but she found she couldn't. She closed her mouth and shook her head. Too many words crowded into her mouth, but she managed to say, "I don't want to lose you either."

He nodded, a hint of a smile curling the corners of his mouth. "Then we'll take it one step at a time, holding onto the fact that we want to be together."

"Sounds good," she said, her voice almost a croak. "Now, I'm starving, and I think you promised me dinner on our wedding day."

"That I did," he said, bringing out the smile in full force now. "Do I have time to shower?"

"Sure," she said, starting the walk back to the farmhouse.

When they arrived, he put his hand on her hip and kissed her again, saying, "I'll be back in thirty minutes. Don't starve, okay?"

"Mm," Sarena said, nearly falling down as he pulled away from her. He walked backward for a couple of steps, a sly, sexy smile on his face. Then he turned and went to his truck, firing up the engine and driving away.

Sarena turned around, as if there'd be a camera crew there to tell her that everything that had happened today had been a joke. No one stood there, and Sarena hurried into the house to get cleaned up for her honeymoon-slash-dinner.

The house was unusually quiet, and she heard the humming of a sewing machine as she went down the hall. "Seren," she said, poking her head into her sister's sewing studio. "Where's Sorrell?"

"She got called into work," Seren said, easing up on the pedal. "How are you?"

"I'm...okay," Sarena said. "We got the chores done, and he ran home to shower."

"You sound excited."

Sarena didn't want to keep lying. It was so exhausting, and she wanted to have someone she could be honest with, because she'd even been fibbing to herself. "I am excited," Sarena said. "I don't want to lose him, and he doesn't want to lose me."

"He said that?"

"More than once."

Seren grinned at her. "So maybe you two can make a real marriage out of this."

"You know what?" Sarena asked. "I'm going to try."

Seren clapped her hands together, though a look of surprise filled her eyes. "Good for you."

"We'll see," Sarena said, immediately pulling on the reins

again. "It's new. We're still new. The marriage certificate means nothing right now." She backed out of the room. "I have to go get ready."

"Have fun tonight," Seren called after her.

Sarena went into her bedroom, the wedding dress she'd laid across the bed almost mocking her. She ignored it and changed her clothes, washed her face, and brushed her teeth. She'd never worn much makeup, but she brushed on some powder to even out her skin tones, added a swipe of mascara and a quick layer of pale pink lipstick. She went out into the kitchen, saying, "Seren, will you—?" She cut off when she saw her sister's panicked face. She held her phone to her ear, and she waved her free hand as if telling Sarena to stop talking.

"No, Aunt Scottie," Seren said loudly. "That wasn't her. She's not here right now."

Sarena didn't dare move, as if her aunt had some sort of radar to sense her movement.

"I don't know why she's not answering her phone. Maybe there's something going on out on the ranch." Seren rolled her eyes, and Sarena hoped Darren wouldn't arrive while Seren was still trying to deflect their aunt.

"All right, well, I have to go. I'll tell her you called and you want her to call you. Uh huh...yep...all right. Bye." She hung up and pressed her phone into the counter. She exhaled as she looked at Sarena.

"What did she want?"

"She heard you were burning fields and selling cattle, and she wanted to know what was going on. Apparently, no one knows about Daddy's will, except for us and Uncle Dale."

"I'll call her," Sarena said. "Tomorrow." She picked up her purse and headed for the front door. "Love you, Seren. Have fun tonight." She opened the door and stepped onto the porch just as Darren pulled up.

A squeal formed in Sarena's throat, and she wanted to run down the steps toward him. She did, not caring that she limped a little bit. And the best part? Darren got out of the truck, laughing as he came toward her too. He swept her into his arms, her feet leaving the ground completely as he swung her around.

Joy filed Sarena, and she wasn't sure she'd ever felt it so keenly before. She hoped she would, and she knew that with Darren at her side, she could. She just had to figure out how to keep him in her life.

CHAPTER 9

Darren looked at himself in the rear-view mirror as he drove along the winding roads through the Hill Country toward the town of Chestnut Springs. He hardly recognized himself, and he definitely didn't know the man who couldn't wait to jump out of his truck to meet a woman. He wasn't sure he'd ever picked a woman up and swung her around. Not even Diana.

Sarena ignited something inside him he hadn't even known existed. He didn't know what it was, but it felt an awful lot like drive. Determination not to let himself slip down into the pit of despair. Desire to wake up every morning without a dark cloud over his head.

Drive, determination, desire.

"Tell me what you're thinking," Sarena said from the passenger seat.

Darren couldn't tell her *exactly* what he was thinking. "I'm thinking I'm starving and want a really good steak. And I'm thinking we should talk about taking a honeymoon."

Sarena made a noise somewhere between a scoff and a gasp, and Darren glanced at her.

"What?" he asked, though he knew what. "You don't like steak? Do *not* tell me you don't eat red meat." He grinned at her, this flirting also something he wasn't well-versed in.

Her face softened into a smile, and she rolled her eyes. "What would the point of a honeymoon be?" She folded her arms and looked out her window, and Darren had enough experience with women to know she wasn't happy with the discussion topic.

"To make it look real," he said. "The marriage. Plus." He drew in a breath and sigh. "I could use a vacation, honestly."

"And what does Darren Dumond do for his vacation?" Sarena asked.

A spark flared through his body. "Darren Dumond would love to see more of the country. Maybe go visit the White House or something like that."

"Do you know how cold it is in Washingon, D.C. right now?" Sarena asked. "It's warm enough here, Darren, but a lot of the country is covered in snow in November and December."

"Well, it's October," Darren said, coming to a stop as the highway from the more rural areas met the street that led to downtown Chestnut Springs. He didn't pull out so he could study Sarena's profile for a moment. "Could you get away from the ranch? For a weekend even."

She turned toward him, and a perfect storm danced through her eyes. "I could," she said. "I have some guys I can call to take over for a bit."

"Will you call them?" he asked.

Sarena watched him for a moment. Then two, and then three. "I can call them tomorrow."

Darren kept his smile from spreading too quickly, and instead let it slowly cross his face. "Great. Let me know, okay? Then I can book something." He made the turn and pointed the truck toward The Longhorn, the best steakhouse in town.

Sarena didn't say much as they arrived, parked, and got a booth in the corner. Darren loved the steakhouse, with the scent of cooking meat and the intimate lights above the tables. He felt like he and Sarena enjoyed plenty of privacy, and he didn't need to look at the menu to know what he wanted.

He lifted it in front of his face anyway, trying to find the right order for his next words.

"We're going to need some rules for this honeymoon," Sarena said, and Darren lowered his menu.

"Rules." He deliberately made sure it didn't sound like a question.

She leaned toward him, and her menu lay perfectly flat on the table. "Yes, Mister Dumond. Rules. We may have a piece of paper that says we're married, but that doesn't mean..." She trailed off, though the fire in her eyes didn't ebb at all.

"You want your own bed," Darren said.

"That's right."

"Can we share a room?"

Sarena sat up and shook her hair over her shoulder. "That would probably be fine."

Darren hadn't imagined sleeping with her on their honeymoon, though he probably should have. "I'm fine with these terms." He reached for the water glass the waiter set on the table.

"You need a few minutes?" he asked.

"We'd like the bacon cheese fries," Darren said. "And the lobster lasagna rolls to start." He glanced at Sarena, who simply stared back at him. "And then, yes, we need a few minutes on our order."

"Drinks?" the man asked, looking at Sarena.

"Diet Coke," she said.

"Same," Darren added.

The man left, and Darren nodded to her menu. "Do you know what you want?"

"How did you know I love the lobster lasagna rolls?"

He hadn't known that, but his heart stuttered out a beat. "I didn't," he admitted. "I just love them, so I ordered them." He smiled at her and reached across the table. "Sarena, can this just not be weird? Like, I get we don't know each other as well as two people who've just gotten married should. I get that. It's fine, though." His mouth felt so dry. Like, desert dry.

But she hadn't pulled her hands away yet, and Darren just needed to get the rest of the words out. "And I want to get to know you. I want to take you to dinner and meet you at the back fence, and learn everything about you. And I don't know." He exhaled, wishing his frustration would go with it.

"Maybe one day, we will find ourselves knowing each other as well as married people do, and maybe..." He shrugged.

"Maybe what?" she pressed.

Darren released her hands and picked up his water glass again. After a few gulps, he looked at her. With his pulse positively pounding in his chest, he said, "Maybe we can make this fake marriage into something real."

There, he'd said it out loud.

Sarena looked like he'd taken his water and thrown it in her face. "Are you serious?"

"Yes."

"Excuse me." Sarena slid out of the booth in one fluid movement, taking her purse with her. Darren didn't know if he should go after her or let her have a few moments. With Diana, he'd learned to give her a couple of minutes to herself. She usually went out to the chicken coops on their ranch, which she'd helped him build with her bare hands. She'd throw feed to the birds and vent to them about whatever was bothering her—which was usually something Darren had said or done. Or something Darren had *not* said or *not* done.

The waiter arrived with their drinks, glancing at the empty bench across from Darren. "Those appetizers should be right out."

"Thank you," Darren murmured. He sat in silence, much the same way he had in the hammock while he waited for Sarena to come back.

She slid into the booth at the same time the waiter set her lobster lasagna rolls on the table. With the flurry of new food and her spreading her napkin across her lap, Darren couldn't meet her eyes.

"Are we ready to order?" the waiter asked.

"I'll have the sirloin," Darren said.

"Market price on that is sixty-nine dollars," the man said.

"That's fine." Darren looked up at him, waiting for the question on his sides. After he gave them, he said, "I'll have the mashed potatoes with mushroom gravy. And the sweet pea salad." He picked up his menu and handed it to the man, who then looked at Sarena.

"I'll have the chicken fried steak," she said. "Same sides."

Warmth and happiness moved through Darren, because he sure did like a woman who would eat fried food.

When they were left alone again, he suddenly had nothing to say. He pulled some cheesy, bacony fries onto his plate while she scooped up one lobster roll. They ate for a moment, and Darren's taste buds didn't care about the hovering cloud of awkwardness at the table. The salty, hot, gooey fries could make anything bearable.

"Darren?"

He looked across the table, barely able to see her under the brim of her cowboy hat.

"I'm willing to see if we can make this marriage into something real."

Darren froze, his hand stalling in midair. "You are?"

She nodded and ducked her head. "I've liked you for months, Darren. Long before I knew about the marriage stipulation in the will."

Darren let her words wash over him and through him,

liking the way the enveloped him in a warm blanket. "All right, then," he drawled. "Let's give it a try."

* * *

"Come on, bud," Darren said into the darkness. His dog came running back to him, and Darren chuckled as he reached down to pat the pooch. "Let's go to bed."

What an exhausting day today had been. His mind seemed to move through every minute as he went up the back steps and into his cabin. He locked the door and turned out the lights.

He'd gotten *married* that morning.

As he looked around his cabin, he realized that nothing had changed. With such a monumental change in his life, shouldn't *something* be different?

But Sarena wasn't here. He'd dropped her off at the farmhouse forty-five minutes ago, taken Koda for a walk, and now... Now he was floundering, right there in the kitchen while his puppy drank from his water bowl.

"No," Darren said, hurrying to lift the bowl off the ground. "It's nighttime, bud. We don't drink right now." He'd have to get up with the pup anyway, and probably sooner now. "Come on." He picked up Koda, cuddling him close to his chest.

Down the short hallway, he set the little dog on his bed and changed into a T-shirt and a pair of basketball shorts. He skipped brushing his teeth and collapsed into bed instead. As tired as he was, he couldn't shut off his mind.

He ran through the wedding luncheon he'd enjoyed with Sarena and her sisters. Hiding out in the barn. Working alongside his wife.

His *wife.*

Their dinner at the steakhouse and discussing a honeymoon, the rules of their relationship, and the easy conversation after that. The kissing at the farmhouse.

"You do like her," he said into the darkness. Koda got up and came to Darren's side of the bed, curling into his hip. And he did like Sarena. He did want to try to make their fake marriage into something real.

He simply didn't know *how* to do that, and he didn't want to hurt her—or get hurt—in the process.

"Dear Lord," he whispered, still getting used to talking to the Lord again. "Help me to know what to do. Bless Sarena so she won't get hurt."

He felt like he should have more to say. He'd heard preachers talk about pouring their souls out to God, but Darren felt like he just had. So he gave one final nod toward the ceiling and closed his eyes.

A moment later, he yanked his eyes open and reached for his phone on the nightstand. He sent a quick text to Sarena. *I'd love to take you to church tomorrow. It starts at ten-thirty. Can you make it work?*

As an afterthought, he added, *I'll help you with your ranch chores afterward, if you need me to.*

He rested the phone on his chest, hoping she hadn't gone to bed yet. If she was anything like he thought she was, he suspected she was doing exactly what he was—lying in bed, unable to sleep, wondering if today had been real or not.

His phone vibrated, and he lifted it to look at it.

Sure, she'd said. *I'd like that.*

Darren grinned at the phone and sent a thumbs-up to her. Finally, satisfied, he put his phone back, patted his dog, and prayed for sleep to come quickly.

CHAPTER 10

Sarena stood back and looked at herself in the mirror. She couldn't decide if the dress looked good on her or not. Yellow always washed her out, despite her tan complexion and dark hair.

"That is the cutest dress ever," Sorrell said, coming into Sarena's bedroom. "Are you going to church?"

"With Darren," Sarena said, turning to get a look at how the skirt fell in the back. She supposed it would work. She hadn't been to church in a while, because the ranch took everything from her most of the time. Working with Darren yesterday had been a dream, and she couldn't help picturing him here, at Fox Hollow, with her.

So much would have to come out for that to happen, and Sarena wasn't ready to face the fallout of that yet.

"I just—" She looked at her feet, remembering why she didn't go to church much. Yes, the ranch required seven-days-a-week work. But when she'd first gone back to church after her accident, everyone had stared at her. Some of the older ladies in the congregation had whispered behind their hands, though they didn't really try to be quiet about the boots Sarena wore with her denim skirt and blue blouse.

Sarena could remember the scenario as if it had happened yesterday. She'd suddenly understood why her father didn't leave the ranch anymore. People sure could be cruel, and Sarena had seriously considered following in her father's footsteps.

But she didn't want to be a hermit on a piece of land somewhere in Texas. She made sure to get to town every now and then to get groceries, attend town festivals, and socialize. She'd been back to church over the years; she just wasn't a regular attendee.

Serendipity entered the room, a pair of cute, tan ankle boots in her hand. "Sorrell said you needed shoes to go with that dress."

Sarena hadn't even realized her sister had left the room. But Sorrell came in behind Serendipity and she sat on the bed. Sarena sat next to her and laid her head against Sorrell's shoulder. "Thanks."

"Try them," Serendipity said. "I'll help you." She knelt down, and Sarena let her pull on a pair of thin socks and then the boots. "They look so good."

Sarena finally let herself look, and she stood up, keeping her hand in Serendipity's until she found her balance. "I think I can walk in these."

"Perfect." Serendipity squeezed Sarena's hand.

"Do you guys want to come to church with me?" she

asked her sisters. Neither of them were dressed, and Sarena suddenly wanted to change back into her sweats and sip coffee, the way Sorrell and Serendipity would while she was gone.

But she felt like she probably needed some help from on high if she wanted to keep Darren in her life, and she did want that. So she'd wear the yellow dress and the ankle boots—and she'd start praying that everyone else would be sick that day, so that she and Darren were the only ones in the congregation that day.

She knew that wasn't going to happen, and she took a big breath. "I don't see anyone jumping up to get dressed." She grinned at her sisters. "Fine. I'm going to get something to eat."

She walked down the hall to the kitchen and had just pulled out a protein shake when the doorbell rang. She took the bottle with her to open the door, her heartbeat suddenly jumping and hopping through her whole body.

Darren stood on the porch, one hand in the pocket of his black slacks. The other pressed against the doorframe, as if the needed it to hold himself up. He wore a white shirt and tie, with yet another dark cowboy hat she'd never seen before.

He was absolutely stunning with the sunshine haloing him, and that sexy smile on his face. "Morning," he said.

"Morning," Sarena repeated, hardly able to believe this man liked her.

"You ready?" He scanned her from head to toe and back, his eyes sparking with desire now. "I like those boots."

"Yeah?" She lifted her left foot, because she couldn't stand on that one alone for very long. "They're Serendipity's."

He reached for her, and Sarena enveloped herself into his arms. He smelled like pine trees and laundry detergent, and Sarena enjoyed the warmth of his body as it seeped into hers.

"You bringin' breakfast with you?" he asked as he stepped back.

"Yes, sir," she said, taking his hand as he turned. They went down the steps together, and he helped her into his truck. None of the awkwardness from last night had followed them home, and Sarena was glad for that.

"Do you want to come back to the ranch for lunch?" she asked.

"Sure," he said. "Then we can work through your chores, and I'm on in the afternoon at Chestnut." He glanced at her. "What did you do last night?"

Sarena looked at him. "After you dropped me off?"

"Yeah."

"Uh..." She folded her arms, her defense for almost everything lately. She figured if she held everything in, she wouldn't give too much away. "I showered and went to bed." And she'd laid awake for a long time. Too long. As if on cue, she yawned, and Darren saw it.

"Didn't sleep well?" he asked.

"Not really," she finally admitted.

"Yesterday was a weird day, right?" he asked. "I couldn't sleep either. Well." He flipped on his blinker. "Once I finally fell asleep, I was fine. It just took forever to actually fall asleep."

"Yeah," Sarena agreed.

The drive to the church happened quickly, and she waited for him to open her door. They went inside hand-in-hand, and the staring had already started by the time Sarena sat on a bench near the back. Darren sat beside her, almost blocking her completely from the view of anyone walking by.

He settled his arm around her shoulders and leaned down, his breath tickling her eat when he said, "No one stares at me like this when I come by myself. You must be real popular."

She giggled quietly and shook her head. "Not true. We're here together, Darren. You didn't know this was going to happen?" She tilted her head back to read his expression, and found their mouths only inches apart. She could kiss him right now as easily as breathing.

But she already felt like a sinner in church, and she wasn't going to actually kiss the man while waiting for the sermon to begin.

"Sarena?"

Every cell in Sarena's body froze. Iciness moved through her, and she seriously hadn't considered the consequences of showing up at church with Darren. Not even a little bit. He'd asked her, which she found sweet. And she wanted to see him. So she'd said yes. Simple as that.

But now, Aunt Scottie stood at the end of the bench, peering past the broad-shouldered cowboy to where Sarena sat in his embrace. "Hey, Aunt Scottie," she said. She took a moment to stand up, a thrill moving through her whole body as Darren steadied her with a hand on her hip as she pressed past his knees to get to the end of the pew.

She hugged her aunt and stepped back. "How are you?"

"Doin' just fine," she said, her words bleeding together the way most Southern women's did. "Who's this?"

"Oh, uh." Sarena turned back to Darren, pure panic racing through her now. "This is Darren Dumond."

"Ma'am." He stood too and extended his hand to Aunt Scottie. She beamed at him like he'd just done the most wonderful thing, and she put her fingertips in his hand as if she were royalty.

Darren knew just what to do with women like her, and he lifted her hand to his lips and kissed the back of her hand. Sarena almost burst out laughing, but she knew better than to do that in church too.

"How do you two know each other?" Aunt Scottie asked, a polite way of trying to get the dirt on Sarena's relationship with Darren.

"We—" Before Sarena could answer, the choir burst into song, everyone's cue to take a seat and get ready for the services to begin.

Aunt Scottie wouldn't want to be out of her seat when she shouldn't be, and she waved at Sarena as she hurried down the aisle to a seat closer to the front. Sarena sat down again too, glad when Darren settled beside her, that arm still around her shoulders. It felt warm and protective, and Sarena hadn't realized she wanted a man at her side, helping and protecting her.

But she did.

"We'll have to run out of here," she whispered to him in the brief moment where the choir stopped singing and the preacher came toward the pulpit. "Unless you want her to know we're married."

"They're going to find out eventually, right?" Darren whispered back.

"Yes," Sarena said. But it didn't have to be today. For some reason, she wanted more time to pass before anyone in her family found out. She wasn't sure what the annulment laws in Texas were, and she'd rather more time passed.

But she couldn't convey any of that to Darren, because the moment she opened her mouth to talk, a woman a couple of rows in front of them turned around and shushed her.

Actually shushed her.

Foolishness dove through Sarena, and she realized why she didn't come to church all that often. Darren's hand on her shoulder tightened, but she kept her face forward until the woman turned around. Then she sagged into Darren's body while he laughed silently. Even getting shushed was better when she was at his side, and Sarena pulled out her phone and quickly typed up her thoughts about why she wanted to keep the marriage a secret from her family for just a little longer.

She tilted the screen so Darren could see it, and he nodded when he finished. He reached over and tapped on her screen for two letters. *Ok.*

Then he added another message. *We'll leave five minutes before it ends.*

Sarena nodded and put her phone away, relieved and already counting down the minutes until she could get out of this chapel.

* * *

THE HOURS BECAME DAYS, and then a week. Then two. Sarena and Darren had fallen into a comfortable routine. They

met in the morning along the back fence. He brought his dog
every time, and Sarena could admit he was cuter than any
other puppy she'd ever seen.

He worked Chestnut Ranch, and she worked Fox Hollow.
Her cowboy contacts had agreed to take the whole ranch for a
weekend, but not for a couple of weeks. Serendipity and
Sorrell went to work as usual. Darren came over for dinner
sometimes, and she went to his cabin sometimes, or they went
out. No matter what, they saw each other in the evenings.

Sarena's favorite nights were the ones with Darren in the
farmhouse with her and her sisters, and then she'd take him
out to the hammock, where they'd talk, plan their trip to
Washington D.C., and kiss.

Oh, how she liked kissing him. She wondered if he knew
how good he was at it, and how inadequate she felt to be
with him.

"So we're leaving on Friday," he said one day, his fingers
moving up and down her arm. He toed the ground every so
often to keep them swaying gently, and Sarena thought she
could fall asleep in his arms and be the happiest woman in the
world.

"Yes," she said. "Three days in the Nation's Capital."

He chuckled and pressed his lips to her temple. "That's
right. I've never been."

"Me either."

"Should be pretty fun then."

"What time is the flight?"

"Eight-ten," he said. "We'll have to leave here by oh, five-thirty. Austin is what? At least an hour. But it's not a huge airport."

"Five-thirty," she said. "Yikes. I don't get up that early in the winter."

"You can sleep in the next day."

"True." She sighed and snuggled deeper into his side. "One more day of work. I can't remember the last time I took off a day from the ranch completely."

"It'll be nice," he said.

"What did you tell the Johnsons?"

"I just said I'd always wanted to go, and if they could spare me, I'd love to make a quick trip of it." He pushed them to get them moving again. "They didn't ask any questions."

"Not a lie," she said.

"Nope." He shifted in the hammock. "What did you tell your cowboys?"

"I asked them if they could take the ranch so I could go out of town. They don't care where I am. They'll get paid."

"True."

They settled into silence, and Sarena had just started to drift somewhere soft and warm when Darren moved. Her eyes shot open, and so many sounds hit her at the same time. Footsteps. The purr of an engine.

Someone saying, "They're right here, Mama. And they're definitely together."

Darren stood up, offering his hand to Sarena. She tried to get her bearings, but her mind spun. The voice finally settled into her ears as she took in the form of her cousin, Regina.

And not far behind her came RonniJean, with a hold on Aunt Scottie's elbow.

She swallowed as she looked at Darren, and he wore a look of resignation that said they were going to have to spill the beans about their marriage.

CHAPTER 11

D arren reached for Sarena's hand and squeezed it. "Hello," he said. "You must be Sarena's cousins. I've heard a lot about you." He extended his hand toward the closest cousin. She sported the same dark hair Sarena did, though hers was much shorter. She also didn't put a quick smile on her face whenever Darren spoke.

"I haven't heard a word about you," she said, her fire and spit directed at Sarena.

"This is my cousin Regina," Sarena said, glancing at Darren. He kept his smile perfectly plastered on his face. He'd had plenty of experience with painting over difficult situations, though he wished he didn't. "And RonniJean. You've met Aunt Scottie, of course."

"Of course." Darren kissed her papery hand again.

"This is Darren Dumond," Sarena said as he shook hands with RonniJena. Regina still had her arms crossed, one hip cocked out. She stood tall and lean, and Sarena must have some height genes somewhere in her family that had skipped her.

He glanced at her, wondering who was going to drop the bomb on them.

"What are you guys doing here?" she asked, her nerves like a scent on the air.

Darren knew exactly why they were there, and he was honestly surprised that he and Sarena had managed to keep their marriage a secret for so long. Two and a half weeks. Not even her cowboys knew, and Darren hadn't said anything to anyone at Chestnut Ranch. Not even Griffin.

"We heard something in town today," Aunt Scottie said, her voice pitching up with importance. "And we've come to see if it's true." She looked from Darren to Sarena. "I think it probably is, but I just can't believe it. My sister would be rolling in her grave."

Sarena said nothing, and Darren determined to follow her lead.

"You didn't invite us to your wedding?" Aunt Scottie asked. "You two *are* married, aren't you?"

"Who told you that?" Sarena asked.

Her aunt made a scoffing sound and looked around the side yard where they stood. "That doesn't matter. What matters—"

"It does to me," Sarena said. She took a step closer to her aunt and cousins. "Did you know that Uncle Dale —nevermind."

Scottie blinked, and Darren got the distinct impression that no, she didn't know anything about Uncle Dale.

"Does he know?" Sarena asked. Darren wasn't sure why it mattered. They'd gotten married legally. Even her uncle couldn't undo their union. They were both of age. Both of sound mind. Both within the limits of Texas law for death or divorce, as well as the waiting period after the marriage license. They'd literally done everything exactly by the law, and no one could challenge the legitimacy of their marriage.

"I don't know if he knows," Scottie said, blinking. "Why didn't you want anyone to know, dear?"

"It's just me being private," Sarena said. "You know how we are. How Daddy was."

Darren didn't, but now wasn't the time to ask. Sarena would tell him later.

Scottie nodded and switched her wise eyes to Darren. How Sarena didn't squirm under the weight of them, Darren didn't know. "So, are you living here, then? Working the ranch with Sarena?"

He wanted to tell her that he had plenty of money and didn't need to work at all. He pulled back on the prideful feelings and just said, "Well…"

"He's moving in when we get back from our honeymoon," Sarena said.

Darren's gaze flew to hers, and he couldn't help the complete shock moving through his system. They hadn't talked about this at all. Not even one word. He knew he looked like this was news to him, and he quickly snapped his mouth shut and ducked his head, using his cowboy hat to hide his face.

"He hasn't moved in yet?" Regina asked.

"He's tying up some loose ends at Chestnut," Sarena said, and Darren groaned inwardly. The Johnsons seemed to know everyone in Chestnut Springs, and if they got dragged into this without even knowing that he'd gotten married... He needed to call Seth immediately.

"So it's taken a week or two," Sarena said. He honestly wasn't sure if they were lying now or not. He hadn't wanted to lie to anyone, and over the course of the last two weeks, they'd talked a lot about being as truthful as possible.

He supposed it had taken a week or two for him to move in. That wasn't a lie. The problem was, he wasn't sure he wanted to move in. He was happy and satisfied with seeing Sarena in the morning and evening, and he thought they had a good system worked out.

Moving in...that would bring a whole new challenge to their relationship. Darren had never lived with anyone he wasn't married to.

And you won't be now either, he told himself, though he knew their marriage wasn't really the kind where man and wife lived happily ever after. *Yet.*

Everyone looked at one another, and the conversation seemed fairly over. Sarena gestured to the house. "Do you want to come in and have some cake? Sorrell made a Boston cream concoction that is delicious."

Darren appreciated her manners, but he really wanted to get back to his cabin and figure out how to tell the Johnsons—

and all the other cowboys at Chestnut Ranch—that he was married.

"Sure," Aunt Scottie said. "Boston cream cake sounds great." She moved toward the front door, both of her daughters following along behind her.

Darren turned to Sarena. "I'm moving in now?" He kept his voice low, but he shot a glance toward her family members. "This is crazy."

"Is it?" Sarena asked, plenty of fire still in her eyes. He actually found it sexy, but he reminded himself he wasn't happy with her. "You're the one who said we should take a honeymoon to make the marriage seem more real."

He'd said that, yes. But he'd also said he simply needed a vacation. Both were true.

"We should've seen this coming," she said. "As soon as Uncle Dale finds out, he'll want to see that the marriage is one hundred percent real." She sighed, and Darren couldn't stay mad at her while she was so crestfallen.

"This is a big thing for me," he said anyway. His anger had dissipated, but he still had a huge amount of fallout to deal with. "I haven't exactly told anyone I'm married. My boss. My friends at Chestnut. This is going to come out of nowhere for them."

"I know." Sarena nodded, and when she looked at him again, she wore bright hope in her eyes. "I can come and explain some things, if you think that will help."

Darren studied her for a long moment. "I don't think we should tell them the reason behind it," he said. "The less people who know that, the better. That way, if Uncle Dale goes to Seth Johnson and asks him about the marriage, Seth won't have to lie." Darren knew Seth wouldn't want to do that.

He probably would for Darren, but it would make him uncomfortable. The Johnsons had literally saved Darren, and he couldn't do anything to hurt them. "I can't stay for cake," he said. "I have to go talk to Seth tonight."

She nodded miserably again, and Darren hugged her. "I'm sorry, sweetheart. I guess we should've thought further down the road." He did hate the word *should've* though. He didn't like thinking about what he should have done, but hadn't.

"You have nothing to be sorry about," she said. "This is my problem, and you're just kind enough to help me with it." She held onto him tightly, and Darren sure did like feeling needed by her. Sarena Adams was so strong, and so capable, that he sometimes forgot she was also human. He loved seeing her vulnerable side, and he appreciated that she liked him and wanted him around.

She stepped back and smoothed down her shirt. "Okay, you go. I'll deal with them."

Darren searched her face for a moment, trying to decide if he could really leave her alone here with her family.

"The gossip mill is running," she said. "If they know, it's possible the Johnsons could hear too. Their parents live in town."

"So do Rex and Griffin," Darren said, another dart of panic hitting him square in the chest. "I'll call you later." He leaned down and kissed her quickly before he strode away, his phone already out.

He tapped the green phone icon as he got behind the wheel of his truck. The line started to ring, and Griffin answered a few seconds later. "Darren, how's it going?" He sounded jovial and glad to hear from Darren, so he couldn't know about the marriage. Yet.

"Griffin," Darren said. "I need to talk to you. And your brothers. Could we set up a meeting?"

"Sounds serious," Griffin said, his voice sobering instantly.

"Yeah," Darren said. "It has to be tonight, too. Like, now." He swung the truck around and got it going the right way down the dirt lane.

"Tonight?"

"Yeah," Darren said. "If possible. People could even call in."

"You're freaking me out. Are you leaving the ranch? I mean, I know you asked for a few days off. You're not going to disappear, are you?"

"No," Darren said. He really didn't want to explain the situation twice. It would be hard enough to vocalize it once. "I'll tell you, but I want to be the one to tell everyone else. So if you'll help me get them together tonight, I'd appreciate it."

"Well, Seth, Trav, and Russ are already out your way," he said. "I can come tonight. So it's just Rex we need to rope into getting out there."

Darren swallowed, his throat so dry and so tight. "I married Sarena Adams," he said. "And I need to move in with her. It's not going to change anything I do at Chestnut, I swear."

Griffin said nothing, and Darren hated the silence filling

the line. It felt huge and overpowering, and Darren could barely breathe through.

"You got married again?" Griffin sounded like he'd taken in a lung full of helium.

"It's a long story," Darren said. "And I can't tell most of it. The bottom line is yes, I got married again, and I'm moving to Fox Hollow as soon as I get back—as *we* get back from Washington D.C."

"Holy cow." Griffin exhaled, and Darren could just see him running his hand through his hair, his eyes wide. "I'll get everyone to the homestead in an hour," he said.

"Thanks, Griffin." Darren's voice threatened to quit on him. "You're a good friend."

"Darren," Griffin said. "If you're in trouble, and you need...I don't even know what. You have more money than I do. But if you need *anything*, I'm here. You're a good man, and we don't want to lose you."

"I'm not in trouble," Darren said, feeling the truth of that way down deep in his soul. "And you're not going to lose me. Like I said, nothing is going to change with me and Chestnut, other than you won't have to pay my room and board anymore. You can put Aaron in my cabin."

"We'll talk more in a bit," Griffin said. "I need to call Rex."

"Okay," Darren said. He ended the call and turned onto the highway to get back to Chestnut Ranch.

He couldn't believe so much could change in such a small amount of time. But he supposed everything had pivoted the moment he'd said, "I will," and that had only taken one second.

Fifteen minutes later, when he pulled up to his cabin, another truck sat there, and he knew he'd find Seth somewhere in the immediate vicinity. Sure enough, Darren slid from the truck at the same time Seth emerged from the shadows on the side of the cabin.

"I got Koda out," he said. "I could hear him whining." The puppy bounded toward Darren, who chuckled as he bent down and scrubbed the canine about the ears.

"Thanks," he said, straightening.

"Griffin said you have something important to tell us." Seth looked at him from under his own cowboy hat, and it was too dark to see his expression.

"Yeah," Darren said. "What else did he say?"

"Nothing, but he sounded a little panicked. I thought maybe I should come see how you were before the meeting."

Darren sighed and moved over to the front steps of his cabin. Koda continued to run around the front yard, and Darren felt bad leaving him home alone at night. "I don't want to explain it a bunch of times," he said.

"Fair enough," Seth said, sitting beside him. "But if there's something I can do, I will."

"I know that." Darren looked at Seth, a fragment of light from the house windows falling on the side of the man's face. "But Millie is due with a baby soon. And Russ has Janelle and his two daughters. Rex just got married." He shook his head. "I know you and Jenna are trying to adopt. I don't want to be a burden. And this isn't going to be a burden. It's not."

"All right," Seth said. "We're meeting at my house, not the homestead. I guess the girls are sick, and Rex won't even go inside the homestead at the moment." He rolled his eyes, which caused Darren to laugh.

"All right," he said as they stood up. "Let's go."

Darren followed Seth over to his house, where Jenna had a plate of brownies on the kitchen counter. Rex, Griffin, and Russ were already there, and they all wore a grim look on their faces.

"It's nothing bad," Darren said in lieu of hello. "Honest." He met Griffin's eye. "You've really worked them up."

"You called at seven-thirty at night and said we had to meet tonight," Rex said. "I was in my pajamas."

Darren rolled his eyes and shook his head. "You're such a liar. I know you stay up late."

"But I could've been." Rex grinned at him and tapped the table, indicating that Darren should come sit down. He did, taking a brownie from the plate. Seth had been smart to bring chocolate.

"So, you're going to wait until Travis comes, is that it?" Russ asked. He didn't seem overly worried, but he was the most laid-back brother.

"Yep," Darren said. "Seth already tried to get me to spill at my cabin. I—it's gonna be hard enough to say it once."

"You just said it wasn't bad," Seth said.

"Yeah," Rex agreed.

"It's not." Darren took a huge bite of chewy brownie so he wouldn't have to talk for a minute. He wished all the Johnson brothers would, and thankfully, Seth said something about one of the fields that had been taking on some flooding, and that got them talking about something else.

Travis entered a few minutes later, yelling, "Sorry," from the front door. "I was literally walking out the door when I dropped a glass, and it shattered everywhere." He entered the kitchen, pausing when he saw them all sitting there. "Okay, so I'm last. What's going on?"

Everyone looked at Darren. He drew in a deep breath, his brownie gone and the moment of truth here. "I'm not quitting," he said. "I want to keep doing what I'm doing at Chestnut Ranch." He looked around at each of them. They were good men, who'd managed to find a way to work their generational land together, despite their wildly different personalities.

They all had wives—almost, because Griffin was still engaged—and families, and Darren counted himself lucky to be at Chestnut Ranch with them.

"I got married a couple of weeks ago," he said, the words scratching his throat. "And I'm moving across the fence to Fox Hollow."

A couple of beats of silence filled the room before Rex asked, "Fox Hollow?"

"Don't the Adams own Fox Hollow?" Travis asked.

"Who'd you marry?" Seth asked. "Ohhh."

"Sarena Adams," Darren said. "And her family just found out, and there's some...complications with that, and I didn't want any of you—or your parents—to hear about the marriage from someone else." He looked around at them again, hoping they knew how much they each meant to him. "That's why I wanted a meeting tonight."

He'd barely finished speaking when Seth's phone rang, and he looked down at it. "It's Mom."

"So she's heard already," Rex said.

Darren's heart fell to his boots as everyone started talking at once. He'd been around the brothers when they acted like this, and he actually liked it. He loved their energy, and the way they just had conversations over one another.

Seth didn't answer the phone, his fingers flying across the screen. "All right, all right," he said. "I told her ten minutes." He waited for everyone to stop talking. "I think Darren's right. This doesn't change anything. His work isn't going to suffer."

"It's really not," Darren said. "I've been sneaking over the fence for weeks—and for a while this summer too." He let a slow smile spread across his face.

"You old dog," Rex said, grinning at him. "Still, I think there's a story to this very secretive marriage."

"Like you can talk," Griffin said, and that shut Rex right down. A moment later, Travis burst out laughing, and Russ joined in. They all did, and Darren felt the tension lighten and then disappear completely.

"So I'll call your mother," Darren said as he stood up. A weight filled his lungs, but he knew once he talked to Sally Johnson, everything would be fine. But if she knew, that meant a whole lot of other people in town did too, and it was only a matter of time before Sarena's uncle found out.

Friday couldn't come fast enough, and Darren seriously considered changing their flight to the following morning instead of having to stay in town for another twenty-four hours.

"Oh, and you'll need to let Aaron, Tomas, and Brian know too," Seth said. "Or do you want me to tell them?"

Darren stumbled as he thought of the men he was closest with on the ranch. "Could you?" he asked. "Although, I'm playing cards with them tomorrow night...I can. I'll take care of all of it." He nodded, pulled his phone out of his back pocket, and started tapping to get to Sally Johnson's number.

CHAPTER 12

Sarena didn't leave the ranch the next day. Darren met her at the fence as normal, kissing her and saying everything went well the night before. All the Johnsons knew about the marriage now, and he was set to move in when they returned from Washington D.C.

They'd worked the day away, texting a lot during lunch. Sarena stayed out of the homestead, just in case Uncle Dale came looking for her. Darren had warned her that he thought the news was all over Chestnut Springs, because Sally Johnson had known. She'd told Darren she'd heard it from a neighbor, but she didn't know where Maurice Lemons had heard it.

"Doesn't matter," Sarena said as she wadded up her garbage and tossed it in the trashcan in the stables. With Sorrell and Serendipity at work, if Uncle Dale came out to the ranch, he'd have to traipse around to find Sarena, or wait.

He wasn't a very patient man, and she hadn't seen him walk more than fifty feet in at least a year. Why he wanted this ranch...she knew why he wanted the ranch. He'd put a FOR SALE sign up the moment the deed was signed over to him, which would guarantee he wouldn't have to work another day in his life. Not that he worked now.

She shook him out of her thoughts and got her afternoon chores done before meeting with her cowboys in the office in the barn. "Okay," she said, entering last. "Sorry to keep you waiting. Did you see Boris is trying to get through that fence again?"

"We oughtta just put him in a calving stall," Phillip said. "We'd all be happier."

"Boris wouldn't be," Sarena said. For some reason, she loved the pigheaded hog. Maybe because he reminded her of herself. "Anyway, I'm leaving in the morning, and I'll be back Monday night. We've got all the normal stuff, and Bryce and Lance will be here tonight." She looked at Theo. "Are we good?"

"Yep," he said, adjusting his cowboy hat. Theo was an excellent cowboy, and he'd worked for her father for three years before Sarena took over the ranch. His family lived in town, but he lived in a small cabin out here, and she knew he had a story behind all of that. She'd just never asked.

Daddy had taught her that it wasn't her business to get involved with the private lives of the cowboys. If they did their job, hers was to leave them alone.

"I heard a rumor," Theo said, looking at her with his bright green eyes. "You and Darren Dumond got married."

Sarena swallowed, wishing just twelve more hours had passed. Then she wouldn't be in town anymore, answering questions she didn't want to answer. "That's right," she said. "He's moving in when we get back from our trip."

Phillip looked to Theo and back to Sarena. "Wow, I didn't know that. Congratulations." He smiled at Sarena, and she managed to return the gesture.

"Thanks." She focused on Theo again. "Can I ask how you found out?"

"My sister," he said. "She works at the pet store, and she said her friend came in and mentioned it."

Sarena nodded. It would be impossible to trace the source of information back to the very first person who'd said it. She knew that. She also knew marriages were searchable online at the county website, and literally anyone could've seen it and called all their besties.

"Is he going to take over the ranch?" Phillip asked.

"No," Sarena said, genuinely surprised by the question. "Why would he?"

"I don't—no, he wouldn't." Phillip glanced at Theo, clearly worried.

"Tell me what you're worried about," she said, watching them both.

"I'm not worried about nothin'," Theo said. "Darren's a good guy."

"I'm not worried about anything either," Phillip said. "Just that I maybe upset you with my question."

"I was just surprised," Sarena said. She trusted these two men. They were close to her age, and they'd worked at Fox Hollow Ranch for a long time. "Darren and I got married to save the ranch," she said simply.

"Sarena," Theo said. "Is it money?"

"Money? No." She shook her head. A sigh slipped out of her mouth. "My father put a stipulation in his will that one of us had to be married—one of us girls—in order to keep the ranch, or it would go to Dale."

"What?" Phillip asked, his eyes widening. "That's insane. Surely your dad didn't do that."

"Yeah, that has Dale Adams written all over it," Theo agreed.

Sarena frowned, trying to think through what they'd said. "Are you saying my uncle somehow...convinced my dad to put that in his will?" She couldn't believe that. "It was from five years ago."

"I don't know," Theo said. "But your dad didn't even talk to Dale." He glanced at Phillip. "We've heard him say lots of negative things about his brother. Why in the world would he ever give Dale the ranch?"

"And why would a marriage be what it would take to keep it?" Phillip asked. He shrugged and shook his head. "It sounds fishy to me, that's all."

Now Sarena thought so too, but she didn't have time to think about it at the moment. "Well, Darren and I got married, and that satisfied the stipulations of the will. The ranch is mine. If Dale shows up while I'm gone, you ask him —respectfully—to leave, and if he doesn't, call Clyde." The police chief who lived five minutes down the road would come help out, she knew that.

"Yes, ma'am," Theo said. "And we'll make sure everything is taken care of here. You go have fun." He gave her a smile and stood up. "Now, I'm going to find out if Sorrell made any more of that cake."

"Wait for me," Phillip said. "That stuff was amazing."

Sarena smiled as they left the office, wondering why Sorrell wouldn't go out with Theo. He wasn't that much older than her, no matter what she said. He'd stopped asking anyway, but Sarena was going to bring it up with Sorrell again. She'd been through the ringer when it came to men, but that wasn't Theo's fault.

Darren wouldn't be coming over tonight, as he had a card game with the other cowboys at Chestnut Ranch. She didn't mind him doing things with his friends, as he'd definitely had a life before they'd met. Not only that, but she had to do laundry and pack tonight, and that couldn't be done if Darren came over.

"You better figure stuff like that out," she muttered to herself, looking at the paperwork she needed to file. She could do it when she returned from her honeymoon.

Sarena couldn't believe this was her life. She'd never dreamed she'd get married, especially after the accident where she'd lost her foot. Surely no one would want a woman with only one foot. That was what she'd told herself for many years. But Darren didn't seem to care at all, which only made him more mysterious and more amazing in Sarena's eyes.

She didn't want to go back to the farmhouse in case Uncle Dale stopped by, but she figured she'd have to face him eventually. "Please not tonight, though," she prayed as she walked back to the farmhouse.

The lights twinkled from the windows, growing larger and

brighter the closer she got. She loved the farmhouse, though it was getting to be older. She could refinish and restain the back deck, protecting the wood and making it beautiful and functional at the same time.

She'd helped her dad repaint only a few years ago, but they could use new flooring in the kitchen, dining room, and living room, and probably some new, updated countertops.

She went up the steps to the back deck, visualizing where she'd stood and became Darren's wife. She opened the back door and went inside, finding Theo and Phillip there, laughing with Seren as they ate Sorrell's cake.

"I've got laundry to do," she said to her sisters.

"You haven't even eaten dinner," Sorrell said. "We kept some soup out for you." She indicated a plastic container on the counter. "Should I heat it up?"

"Yes, please," she said. "I'll get a load going and come join you guys." She loved having the cowboys over in the evening, and they hadn't stopped by for a couple of weeks.

Since she'd been spending more time with Darren. So maybe they had stopped by, and she'd just missed them because she'd been in the hammock, kissing her husband.

Sarena's face heated for some reason, and she hurried down the hall to her bedroom to get her dirty clothes.

Laundry was one of the easiest chores Sarena had to do, and she absolutely hated it. So her basket positively overflowed, and she could barely heft it to get it down a couple of doors to the washing machine.

She'd have to figure out how to do household things, pay bills, and eat dinner with Darren around, as he would be moving in. She put in a couple of laundry pods, loaded the machine as full as she dared, and started it, her mind whirring around where in the world Darren would sleep.

The only other bedroom in the homestead was her father's, and Sarena hadn't been inside since his death.

She went back that way now, pausing outside the closed door. She didn't know if Sorrell or Serendipity had been inside, or what she'd encounter when she opened the door.

Her heart pulsed, sending vibrations through her whole body. She couldn't go inside. It was her *father's* room. She couldn't just give it to Darren.

"Yes, you can," she whispered. He had to have somewhere to sleep, and the only reason he was moving in was because of Daddy's ridiculous will.

He could provide a bedroom for the husband Sarena had had to procure.

She pressed her lips together and opened the door, met with a fresh, crisp scent she'd literally never smelled in this room before. Someone had definitely been in here, as everything had been cleaned, pressed, folded, stretched, and sanitized.

The blinds were open, and Sarena could imagine the sun streaming through the slats in the morning. The bed looked completely different, though it was the same. The headboard still went halfway up the wall, but the dark blankets were gone, replaced by a downy, white comforter that looked like puffy clouds.

The carpet had been vacuumed, and Sarena stepped inside the room. A family picture from a couple of years ago sat on the dresser, but all of Daddy's change, his loose bills, and his belts were gone. She stepped over to the dresser and opened the top drawer, finding it empty.

All the drawers were empty. The closet didn't hold a stitch of clothing or a single pair of shoes.

Sorrell and Serendipity must've done this at some point since Daddy's death. Sarena wondered when, and then where they'd put all of their father's things.

Surely they hadn't thrown it all away. She hoped they hadn't, at the same time she was extremely happy she hadn't had to go through any of it.

Tears sprang to her eyes as she ran her fingertips along the windowsill. There wasn't a particle of dust anywhere.

"She's in here," Serendipity said.

Sarena turned toward her. "Did you do this?" She hated the weakness in her voice, but at the same time, it was okay to miss her father. And miss him she did, powerfully, in that moment.

"Sorrell and I did," she said as Sorrell arrived in the doorway too.

"When?" Sarena asked.

"A while ago," Sorrell said. "We boxed up a bunch of stuff and put it in the back shed. Some stuff we threw away." She glanced at Seren. "Are you mad?"

"No." Sarena shook her head, dislodging some tears. She surveyed the room again and looked at her sisters. "I'm grateful. And I miss him so much."

"I know." Sorrell said, coming into the room and gathering Sarena into a hug. "I do too."

"We all do." Seren made a three-way hug, and Sarena always felt stronger and better when she stayed close to her sisters.

"And now the room is ready for Darren," Seren said. "Right? Or is he going to sleep in your bedroom?" She stepped back, questions in her eyes.

"He'll be in here," Sarena said. "We're not...I mean, we're getting along great, but we're not ready for that." In reality, Sarena wasn't sure what Darren was ready for or not. But she knew she wasn't in love with him, and she'd never wanted to be intimate with a man she didn't love—and who didn't love her.

Darren handled her with care, no doubt about that. But he hadn't said he loved her, and Sarena couldn't imagine doing more than a little kissing, despite the marriage certificate.

"Come eat," Sorrell said. "Then you can pack for your amazing honeymoon." She grinned at Sarena, and together, they went down the hall to the kitchen. She tried to put Darren into the situation in the kitchen, and she could see him there. Easily.

She hoped he felt the same—that he fit here—when he moved in next week.

* * *

THE NEXT MORNING, Sarena stood on the front porch, her packed and ready suitcase beside her. Uncle Dale hadn't shown up, and Sarena thought she might be able to make it out of town without having to deal with him.

A truck's engine came down the lane, and relief filled her when the blue and white vehicle rounded the corner. She met Darren in the driveway, and he put her bag in the back of his king cab, helped her in the front seat, and got behind the wheel.

"How was last night?" he asked.

"Great." She looked at him. "You? How did cards go?"

"Oh, it was swell." He flashed her a smile, and then he leaned toward her. "Kiss me?"

Sarena always wanted to kiss him, and she scooted across the seat a little and met his mouth with hers. "Cards must've gone bad," she murmured. "Did you lose a bunch of money?"

"No." He kissed her again, and Sarena liked the way his hand drifted down the side of her face and curled around the back of her neck. "I had to tell the guys about us, and then there were a lot of questions."

"Mm." Sarena pulled away.

"I'm tired of the questions," he said, straightening and pulling his seatbelt across his body.

"You and me both."

"So no questions this weekend," he said, looking at her. "Deal?"

"Deal."

"Great." Darren put the truck in gear and swung around, only to come face-to-face with her uncle's truck.

Sarena's heart froze but still struggled to beat against the icy cage. "Keep going," she said.

Darren did, easing to the right, the truck going off the road to go around Uncle Dale.

"Don't stop," she said. "Don't roll down your window."

Thankfully, Darren kept moving, leaving her uncle in the rear-view mirror. Neither of them spoke, and he made it to the highway and turned toward Austin, accelerating quickly.

Sarena watched the mirror, expecting Uncle Dale to come roaring up behind them.

He didn't.

Sarena felt like she'd dodged a bullet—but she was on her way to the airport to begin her honeymoon with her new husband, so she still had plenty of obstacles to watch out for.

CHAPTER 13

D arren couldn't believe how cold it was in Washington D.C. He'd thought he'd packed well enough, with a jacket and a pair of gloves. But he needed a coat.

So the first thing he'd done once he and Sarena had realized how Texan they were—which was code for "unprepared" —was buy them new coats, hats, scarves, and gloves.

Sarena had stood there and let him, and Darren knew he needed to have a conversation with her about money.

He just didn't want to do it on their honeymoon. He wanted to enjoy his time seeing the sights, so he kept his hand in hers and said, "Our tour is in forty minutes."

"I can't wait," she said. "This place is *amazing*." She looked around, seemingly trying to take everything in at once. Darren knew he was trying to. He'd never lived in a big city like this before, and the sheer number of people was overwhelming.

He knew he stuck out with his cowboy hat, as several people glanced at him as he and Sarena walked down the street. But no one had said anything.

He hailed a cab, actually surprised that just throwing up his hand had worked. "We've got a tour at the White House," he told the driver, holding the door for Sarena. He climbed in afterward, and off they went. He felt like someone had poured magic into his veins, because he'd never ridden in a cab before.

Ten minutes later, he paid the guy, got out, and only a few steps away was the entrance for tours. "That was easy," he said.

"Were you expecting it to be hard?" she asked.

"A little." Darren sure did like the cute hat Sarena wore, with her dark hair spilling out the bottom of it. "I mean, I've never ridden in a cab before."

"Me either." She glanced down the road where the yellow car had gone. "That was exciting."

They smiled at each other, and Darren reached for her. Their flight had gone well, and the only thing they were doing this afternoon was the tour. Then they'd check into their hotel, and Darren had done some research for the best restaurants in the city. He'd booked a reservation for seven-thirty, and he hadn't allowed himself to think past that.

"Let's take a picture," she said, swiping on her phone to make the camera change directions. He pressed his face close to hers, and she snapped the selfie of the two of them, the White House behind them. "Aw, we're so cute," she said.

"Send that to me, would you?" he asked. "I should probably send it to my mother. Let her know what's going on."

"Your mother?" Sarena asked.

"Yeah," Darren said. "Both of my parents are still alive." He hadn't spoken about his family much, because there had been so much going on. "I have two sisters too. They're both married. One of my brothers is, and the other isn't. And then there's me."

"Where do they live?"

"My parents are still in Frio," he said. "I don't get down there to see them as much as I should." He could picture the small home where they lived—where he'd grown up. The miles of fields surrounding them. The river raft tours he'd worked growing up. "One of my sisters is in Concan. The other is in Llano. Both of my brothers still work my father's ranch."

"You're a Hill Country family," she said, smiling.

"That we are." He edged forward with the line, finally giving the guard his name. They got to go through the yellow rope with several others, and a few minutes later, someone came out and allowed them to come inside, claiming the weather was unusually cold for this time of year.

Darren was glad to hear that, because he didn't want to admit he hadn't even checked the weather before leaving Texas. "No word from your sisters?" he asked.

"Nothing." Sarena didn't check her phone. "They'll deal with it."

Darren nodded, a knot of unrest in his gut. He tried to find the source of it, and he knew what it was. As much as he didn't want to have hard conversations on their honeymoon, he needed to come clean with her about his money.

"Sarena," he said, pulling her away from the couple standing nearby. "I have to tell you something."

Her eyes grew worried as they searched his. "Okay. What's wrong?"

"Nothing's wrong." He just wished he didn't have to have this conversation. "So, I know you probably don't care, but it's something I've been thinking about. And I want you to know."

"Okay," she said again, her voice wary now.

"I...have a lot of money in the bank." He cleared his throat and glanced around. No one seemed to care about him and Sarena at all. "When I sold the ranch my wife and I had bought, it was to a major oil company. They paid me a lot of money for the land." He swallowed, unsure of why his money brought him so much anxiety.

"You look like you're going to throw up," Sarena said, lifting her hand to cradle his cheek. "Why is this a hard thing to tell me?"

"I don't know," he said.

"Because having a lot of money shouldn't make a man break out into a sweat." She gave him a sweet smile that made Darren's soul light up. "But thank you for telling me." She tipped up onto her toes, and Darren put his hands on her waist, because he knew she couldn't stand like that for long. Their kiss was sweet and short, because their guide arrived.

As he welcomed them to the White House and started giving safety instructions, Sarena whispered, "How much is a lot?"

"Nine figures," he said.

"Is that...?" She looked at him, her eyes wide. "Billions?"

"Yes," he confirmed, nudging her forward so they wouldn't be the last ones to officially start the tour. And with that juicy piece of gossip out of the way, Darren was finally able to relax and enjoy the tour.

He'd never seen anything like the White House, and he found himself wanting to stay longer in each room, really examine every dish, and talk to every person there.

"That was *incredible*," he said as they left. "The whole trip was worth it, just for that." He looked at Sarena. "What did you think?"

"I think you're right," she said. "That really was amazing." She exuded only happiness, and that made Darren happy.

They took another cab to the hotel, and Darren stepped up to the ritzy counter to check-in. He gave his name and said they'd stowed their bags from earlier in the day. The woman sent someone to get them, and she handed Darren a keycard with all the pertinent instructions for the gym, the swimming pool, and the Wi-Fi.

His heart started to flail in his chest as their bags arrived and they walked toward the elevators. He hadn't told Sarena about what type of room he'd booked, and it should have two bedrooms, with two beds. He'd been thinking about their sleeping arrangements for days, not just for this trip but for when he moved into the farmhouse too. Griffin had offered to help with the move, and while Darren had tried to put him off, Griffin wouldn't be dissuaded from coming to help.

Darren couldn't have him put all the boxes in a separate bedroom, but he didn't know what to do.

"Here we are," he said, arriving at the corner suite. The keycard worked smoothly, and he entered the cool, dark room. It smelled like lilacs, and he took a deep breath as he towed his suitcase inside.

"It's huge," Sarena said from behind him.

"It's a suite," he said, flipping on a light to reveal the living room, complete with two couches, a TV, and a table in it.

"Good thing you told me about the money," Sarena said. "Because I would've asked here. I mean, look at this place. It's bigger than my house."

"Oh, come on," he said with a laugh. "It is not. It's bigger than my house, but that's not hard to do." A small kitchen area, with a huge dining room table sat to his left. Just behind that was the bathroom, and then one of the bedrooms.

"So there's a bed there," he said. "And one right here." Beyond the living area was another king-size bed, and Darren figured he'd take that one. "You can have the bedroom."

"Okay." Sarena went that way, her suitcase putting wheel-lines in the carpet behind her. Darren watched her go, feeling a little disappointed. About what, he didn't know.

A yawn pulled through his body and came out of his mouth. "We have time for a nap," he called as he went past the couches and the TV. "Our dinner reservations aren't until seven-thirty."

"Okay," Sarena said from far away.

Darren kicked off his boots, glad to have them off his feet, and left his suitcase near the foot of the bed. He laid down, a long groan coming from his mouth. He took off his cowboy hat, setting it on the nightstand beside the bed, and closed his eyes.

He must've been really tired, because the next thing he knew, someone had woken him. He hadn't even realized he'd fallen asleep.

"Can I lay by you?" Sarena whispered. "This place is too big."

"Sure," Darren said sleepily, not really sure why she thought this hotel room was too big. He'd been to the farmhouse, and that kitchen, dining, and living area was massive.

She curled into his side, and Darren lifted his arm around her. A happy sigh moved through him, and he couldn't believe what an amazing day today had been.

"Love you, Sarena," he whispered just before drifting off to sleep again.

* * *

"Yes, that goes," he said a few days later. The honeymoon had passed so quickly, and Darren yearned to run away with Sarena again. They'd had a great time in Washington D.C., and Darren's feelings for her had multiplied many times. He felt right on the edge of falling all the way in love with her, and he'd dug in with both feet to keep himself from doing that.

Sarena seemed to like him too, and for that, he was grateful. But he knew they still had a long way to go before their marriage was real.

She'd slept in the same bed with him in Washington D.C.,

which he'd found strange. When he'd asked her about it, she said she didn't want to be in that big bedroom all alone. With a king-sized bed, there'd been plenty of room for both of them, and Darren had simply held her close to his heartbeat as they'd drifted to sleep. He'd thought he wouldn't be able to sleep with her so close, but the opposite had been true.

He fell asleep faster and slept better with her at his side. Nothing had happened beyond a good-night kiss, and Darren was okay with that for now.

He didn't want to pressure Sarena, and she'd been a bit nervous with him that first night at dinner. She hadn't slipped into bed with him until halfway through the night, and by the next morning, she'd been back to normal.

Darren was learning that each day, he had to come up with a new definition for normal. Today's normal was him moving from one ranch to another, all in one trip, with just two pickup trucks.

Griffin followed him, and Darren's nerves grew and clashed within himself the closer to Fox Hollow he got. Finally, he parked in front of the farmhouse, as he had many times before. No one stood on the porch to welcome him, and he wished Sarena was there. He liked seeing her there, waiting for him when he pulled up.

With his heart thumping almost painfully in his chest, he turned to go to the back of his truck. Griffin eased to a stop beside him, but Darren couldn't look at him. He slid a couple of boxes to the end of the tailgate and hefted them into his arms.

If he could get into the house first, maybe he could have a

quickly whispered conversation with Sarena. But he didn't know how to walk away from Griffin, who was just getting out of his truck.

Help, he thought, and something popped into his head.

"You can just start stacking them on the front porch, if you want," Darren said. "I'll take them in."

"You got it," Griffin said, and relief cascaded through Darren like a waterfall. He'd just stepped onto the porch when the front door opened.

"Hey," Sarena said. "You said you were going to call when you left."

"Oh, I forgot." He smiled at her, pausing in front of her. "Look, I didn't tell him this was a..." He cleared his throat, his heart beating so dang hard. "Sort of fake thing. Can I just put these boxes in your room? I'll move them once he's gone."

"Of course," she said. "I guess you didn't see the car parked on the side of the house?" She wore worry in her eyes too. "My aunt and cousins are here."

"Perfect," he said under his breath. "Okay, kiss me, and I'll get this stuff taken in."

Sarena stretched up and kissed him, and while Darren had wanted to do it so everyone could see, it was also a very real connection for him. He hoped for Sarena too, but he had no way of knowing.

He broke the kiss quickly and turned back to Griffin. "Have you met Sarena Adams?"

"I'm sure I have," Griffin said, coming all the way up the steps and shaking her hand. He smiled easily as Darren introduced him. "Nice to meet you."

"And you. Thanks for helping Darren this morning."

Darren had all kinds of eyes on him, and he just wanted to get this move over with. Pronto.

Sarena stepped back, and he went past her and into the house. "Last bedroom on the left," she said, and Darren acknowledged all the women in the kitchen with a nod of his head. With Sarena, there were now six women here. And as soon as Griffin left, just one man.

Darren felt like he carried the weight of the world from the front porch to Sarena's bedroom over and over again, the dread in his gut only adding to the heaviness in his footsteps. He'd just tossed several garment bags with his jackets and suit coats onto Sarena's bed when he heard laughter coming from down the hall.

He went back that way to find Sarena had invited Griffin in, and she was serving sweet tea and muffins for breakfast. His stomach roared for food at the same time his brain recoiled at the thought of eating.

Griffin laughed with the ladies in the kitchen, able to fit in seamlessly. Darren envied the man who seemed to have everything going for him at the moment. He stepped to Sarena's side and slipped his hand into hers. She glanced at him, her laughing eyes matching the genuinely happy smile on her face.

And Darren's worried and dread dried right up. Maybe moving in together wouldn't be so bad after all.

"Got it all?" she asked.

"Yep," he said. "You'll have to help me with the unpacking, so I know where I can put things."

"Sure thing." She picked up a plate and handed it to him.

"I'm sure you didn't eat breakfast. Sorrell made her world-famous cranberry corn muffins."

"World-famous, please," Sorrell said.

"They are," another cowboy said he held the back door for a second one to come in. He smiled at Sorrell, who ducked her head and tucked her hair. Darren had seen women do that before, and he sensed a romance between Sarena's sister and the cowboy.

"You remember Theo and Phillip," Sarena said. "Right, Darren?"

"I've met them once or twice." He put down his plate and shook hands with the two cowboys, thankful for more testosterone in the farmhouse. "And this is Griffin Johnson, from Chestnut." More handshakes, and then Theo picked up a plate too.

"Oh, Sorrell," Theo said, his voice filled with a tease. "You're tryin' to get me to propose, aren't you?" He picked up a pair of tongs and then something from the stove Darren hadn't seen yet. "I mean, candied, bacon-wrapped sausages?" He grinned from ear to ear as he turned, his plate stacked with the meat candy. "I love these."

He moved over to where Sorrell sat at the huge dining room table. He pressed a kiss to the top of her head. "I love you." He sat down, that smile still in place, and started eating.

Everyone else seemed to be frozen, especially Sorrell, and Darren knew his heart was sprinting with those last three words Theo had said.

"Oh, wow," Griffin said, with something obviously in his mouth. "I see what he means. I might have to break off my engagement with my fiancée and marry you instead, Sorrell."

Darren sputtered out a chuckle, and it grew into a proper laugh, effectively breaking the tension in the kitchen. "I guess I need to try these candied bacon-wrapped sausages." He picked up his plate and moved over to the stovetop, where a sheet pan of miniature sausages, definitely wrapped in bacon, with plenty of melted brown sugar, waited.

He could put the whole thing in his mouth, and when he did, a party started. A moan followed quickly, and he enjoyed the salty sweetness. "That's it," he said. "I better move my boxes into Sorrell's room."

"Oh, stop it," Sarena said, swatting his bicep as everyone laughed, Darren included. He allowed his fantasies to race ahead for the first time since he and Sarena had started down this journey of a fake marriage.

CHAPTER 14

Sarena linked her arm through Darren's as he stood at the stovetop. "Theo's asked Sorrell out at least a dozen times," she said very quietly. So quietly that he had to lean down to hear her. "She says no every time."

"Oh, gosh," he said. "I didn't know."

"You and Griffin did the exact right thing." She looked at him, his face only inches from hers. "Thank you, Darren." She didn't know how to properly articulate how grateful for him she was. Could he feel it in her touch, in her kiss? She hoped and prayed he could.

She tipped her head back a bit more and kissed him, pouring everything she had into the touch.

"Thank you," she whispered again, stepping back before she made a scene by making out with him in the kitchen, in plain view of everyone at the table several yards away. She put a few sausages on Darren's plate for herself, along with another muffin.

They joined everyone at the table, and Sarena let the conversations wash around her and through her while she ate. The food felt like lead in her stomach, because she normally drank breakfast and called it good.

Finally, Griffin stood up and said, "I better get back. I'll see you tomorrow, Darren."

"Yep." Darren waved to his friend. He hadn't eaten much at breakfast either, and he'd said even less than her. She needed to get everyone out of the farmhouse right now.

"Okay, I'm off to work," Sorrell said, standing up. She already wore her pressed gray slacks and her hair just-so. She worked as a director at the community center, and that meant a lot of meetings, sometimes with important people around Chestnut Springs.

"We better head out too," Theo said, his plate empty now. "Since Sarena is taking *another* day off work." He gave her a playful smile and took his plate to the kitchen sink before hurrying after Sorrell. Phillip followed him at a much slower pace, and Sarena got up when everyone else did, trying to ignore the whole situation with Sorrell and Theo.

She hadn't said anything to her sister about accepting a date from the man, because Sorrell was almost forty years old, and she could make her own decisions. Sarena knew what it felt like to have a crack right down the middle of her soul, and she wished Sorrell didn't have a past as potholed as Sarena's. But she did, and she'd have to deal with that on her own terms.

"We'll let you two get settled," Aunt Scottie said, leaning over to give Sarena a kiss on both cheeks.

"Thanks for coming, Aunt Scottie," Sarena said, though

she hadn't invited her aunt or her cousins. Darren got the same hug and kisses, and he trailed one step behind her while her family left.

Sarena gripped the door as they all walked out, finally meeting Seren's eye. "Wow," she said.

"Yeah." Sarena sighed. "You have a late tour tonight, right?"

"Yes, the five-thirty," she said. "I'll be back around eight."

Sarena suddenly didn't want her sister to leave. Or maybe she did. She didn't know which way was up at the moment, to be honest. Serendipity left, and Sarena closed the door behind her, automatically pressing the lock and turning the deadbolt.

She faced Darren, who waited only a few feet away. "Did you get the day off at Chestnut?"

"Yes."

"So...should we go get you unpacked?" Sarena would rather stay busy. If she worked, she didn't have to think so hard about everything that had changed in her life in the past month.

"I can do it," he said, but she followed him down the hall and into her bedroom anyway. He didn't have a whole lot, and Sarena wondered what her life would look like if she had to pack it all up too.

Probably about the same. Clothes, jackets, a couple of pillows, shoes—cowboy boots for Darren—toiletries, and a few dishes.

He didn't pick anything up and turn to leave the room. Instead, he reached into a box that didn't have a top and pulled out a picture frame. "Do you want to see Diana?"

Sarena moved to his side, her muscles squeezing tight. She looked at the woman in the picture frame, and she seemed so full of life. "She's very pretty," she said. Diana had hair the color of copper, with laughing eyes that could be brown or green, or a bit of both. She didn't look like Sarena at all, and that brought a hint of comfort to her heart.

"She looks so happy here," Darren said. "Because we'd just signed on the ranch." His voice sounded like a shadow of the one he normally spoke in.

"I'm so sorry," Sarena said. She stood right next to him, but they weren't touching. She felt close to him, but also terribly far away. "How did she die?"

"There was an accident at the mill where she worked," he said. "Five people died that day; she wasn't the only one."

"The only one that mattered to you," Sarena said, gently putting her hand around Darren's as he held the picture frame. He'd said he loved her while they were in Washington D.C.

She knew he didn't remember saying those words. But Sarena also knew without a shadow of a doubt that he'd said them. At first, she'd thought she'd hallucinated. She'd asked him what he'd said. But he'd already fallen back asleep. They'd gone to dinner, and then that night, Sarena hadn't been able to sleep in the other bedroom, the bed too big, the idea of Darren in the other room too much for her to handle. Especially if he really did love her.

She'd waited, hoping he'd bring it up so they could talk about it. But he never had, and that was when Sarena knew he hadn't realized what he'd said. Darren didn't normally shy away from hard conversations, including this one about his late wife.

"Darren." She took the picture from him, and he let her. His eyes looked like shiny marbles when they met hers, and Sarena's whole heart and soul ached for him. "Do you remember when we first got to our hotel room in D.C.?" She set the picture lovingly back into the box on the bed.

His eyebrows drew down, and Sarena wanted to smooth away all of his troubles. She'd never felt like that about anyone besides her sisters, and she didn't know what it meant.

"We took a nap," he said. "Before dinner."

"Yeah," she said, sliding her hands up his arms and adding, "I'm going to take off your hat." She knew most men didn't want anyone touching their cowboy hat, and Darren stiffened as she removed his from his head, but he let her. She set it carefully in the box on top of the picture. "You said something before you fell asleep, but I don't think you remember saying it."

His hands came to her waist, and Sarena wanted to stand within the circle of his arms forever. She knew then that she loved him. "What did I say?" he asked.

"You said you loved me."

His eyes widened, but he didn't run. He didn't deny it.

She ran her fingertips down the side of his face. "Is that true?" She desperately wanted it to be true. She let her eyes close, and then she could just experience him in his rawest form. The scent of him, the feel of his strong hands on her back, almost the taste of him if he'd just lean down and kiss her. "Because I'm in love with you."

She heard him inhale through his nose, but she didn't open her eyes. Saying such intimate things to him was much easier if she didn't have to see his reaction.

"Yes," he said, his breath brushing her cheek as he leaned closer. "It's true."

Sarena tucked herself against his chest, pure joy moving through her. She'd never been loved by a man like him, and she just wanted to bask in the glow of it for a moment. Tears pressed behind her closed eyes, but she kept them at bay. "Then maybe you don't need to move across the hall," she finally said.

"Maybe I don't."

Neither of them moved, and she wondered what he was thinking. She'd asked him in the past, but she didn't now. A tremor moved through her body, though she wasn't cold.

"You okay?" he asked.

"I'm scared out of my mind," she admitted.

"Yeah?" Darren shifted, easily moving to kiss her. "Why's that?"

Sarena trembled again just thinking about doing more than kissing with him. What would she tell her sisters? Had she really fallen in love with him in only three weeks? Could he really have fallen for her that fast too?

What if he was too good to be true?

She didn't have any answers for any of her questions, so she focused on kissing Darren back. He kept things slow and sweet, despite Sarena's almost panicked movement. He finally pulled away, and Sarena opened her eyes. "It's okay," he said. "You—we don't have to do anything."

"You don't remember saying it, do you?" she asked.

He shook his head slowly. "No, but it doesn't matter." He pressed his lips to her forehead. "I can *feel* it. I *am* in love with you too."

"I've never been in love before," Sarena admitted.

"It feels good, doesn't it?" he asked.

A smile slipped across her face. "Yeah."

He stepped back, and Sarena didn't like that. He pulled in a long breath. "All right. So I'll stay in here with you?" He raised his eyebrows and made the sentence sound like a question.

"Yeah." She nodded and looked at his boxes and garment bags. "Yeah, I think that will work just fine."

They started unpacking, and Sarena mostly moved things in her closet so Darren could put his jeans and shorts in a few of the drawers in her closet organizer. He put his boots on the shoe rack, and the next time Sarena went into the closet, she simply stared at them.

This was very real all of a sudden. This was happening. Had happened.

She turned and looked at him as he broke down one of the last boxes that had held his things. What was she going to do with him once it was time for bed?

She shivered again, her mind reeling with all they could be. She noticed that he hadn't taken his wife's picture out of the box, and she hadn't seen where he'd put it. Surely he wouldn't throw it away. Diana was part of his past, the same way Sarena's injured foot was. He shouldn't have to hide it.

Sarena reached down and took off her shoes and socks,

then her prosthetic. She could walk without it, and she was actually more comfortable without it on.

"Do you just have the one?" Darren asked, startling her. She almost dropped the prosthetic as she was reaching to put it in the case where she kept it when she wasn't wearing it.

"Yes," she said. "They're really expensive."

"Good thing you married a cowboy billionaire," he said, that handsome smile crossing his face. He reached for her, and she willingly entered his arms. "What do you want to do now?" he asked. "I'm unpacked. It's not even noon yet, and we have the whole day off."

Sarena had a few ideas, and one of them terrified her greatly. But she loved Darren. She trusted Darren. He loved her. They were married...

She lifted up on only five of her toes and kissed him, hoping he'd get the idea for the first thing she wanted to do that day. By the way he kissed her back, she was pretty sure he did.

CHAPTER 15

Darren woke up the next morning, the room still pitch black. Only a moment passed before he realized he wasn't sleeping in a bed with Koda at his side. No, the warm body next to him was his wife, and Koda now had a spot near his feet.

A smile trickled through him as he thought about everything that had happened in the past twenty-four hours. He had a new home. A new place to hang his hat. A new bed to sleep in, with a pretty wife who loved him.

He listened to Sarena breathe in slowly, and then out. They'd consummated their marriage yesterday, and Darren waited for the guilt to gut him.

It didn't come. He didn't feel the need to apologize to Diana for anything.

Maybe you really have moved on, he thought, only a moment before his alarm sang out. Beside him, Sarena groaned, and he quickly sat up to silence the alarm.

"What time is it?" she asked grumpily.

"Five-thirty," he said. "I always get up at five-thirty."

"You're too cheerful about that." She swatted him with a pillow, and Koda came up from the foot of the bed.

"No, bud," he whispered. "Come on back down here. I'm getting up." He swung his legs over the side of the bed, but the puppy simply took his spot instead of going back to where he'd been sleeping.

He showered in Sarena's bathroom, got dressed, and went around to her side of the bed. "I'll see you at the fence later?"

"Mm hm," she said, tilting her head up for a kiss. Darren kissed her, acknowledging the powerful feelings moving through him.

"All right," he said before he let himself get out of control. "Love you, Sarena."

"I love you too," she said. He watched her snuggle deeper into the covers, and then he looked at his puppy.

"Come on, Koda," he said, but the dog didn't move. "What? You're going to sleep late with her?"

"I'll bring him to the fence," Sarena said, one hand snaking out from underneath the blankets to stroke Koda's side.

"Unbelievable," Darren said, but he smiled all the same. He left, walking down the hall to the kitchen, realizing he'd have a few minutes every morning to himself to make coffee. His routine at his own cabin had been the same, and he sure did like that not everything in his life had been upended when he'd agreed to marry Sarena.

And the things that had changed were good. "They are,"

he told himself. "Today is a great day." He didn't even have to work that hard to convince himself of it.

Only a slip of anxiety moved through him, and only when he saw the time and realized he should've left ten minutes ago to get to Chestnut Ranch on time. He muttered to himself as he left the farmhouse, and he drove faster than he would've. He didn't want to be late after Seth had so graciously given him time off for a honeymoon, and then to move.

Honestly, though, Darren had taken more time off in those four days than he had in the previous four years he'd worked at the ranch. Still, he hated being the last one to get to his post for the day, and that had definitely happened today.

He kept his head down as he went through stable number three, checking the horses and moving the ones who needed stall cleanings. He did the work, pitching in new straw and cleaning water troughs, just like always.

His phone buzzed, but he didn't check it. He'd never been tied to his device before, and he wasn't going to start now. Something nagged him in the back of his head, and he finally did pull out his phone to see who'd texted.

Seth: Lunch at Travis's homestead today. Everyone is invited.

Darren loved days where he got to eat at Travis's. His wife, Millie, was an excellent cook, and Darren usually left with at least one container of whatever she'd made. Then he'd eat well for another meal.

Buoyed by this development, he finished in the stable and went to get the ATV. He had no reason to drive the thirty minutes to the back fence, but he'd been doing it for weeks without a reason. His chores hadn't suffered, and no one had even known.

Today, though, Rex caught him just as he was about to enter the equipment shed. "Hey, Seth has a ton of dogs out. He wants us all over to the enclosures to help."

"All right." Darren switched directions, going with Rex in the opposite direction of the ATVs and the back fence. And his wife.

He knew that he couldn't keep every promise he made. Was meeting at the back fence a promise? He wasn't sure. He knew it took Sarena thirty minute to walk out there, and if he wasn't going to meet her, he should tell her. So he quickly dashed off a text to her, looking up as the sound of barking met his ears.

So much barking.

"He has too many dogs," Rex grumbled. "Hey, where's Koda?"

"Oh, uh, Sarena kept him this morning."

Rex gave Darren a hard look, but Darren didn't understand the meaning behind it. At least ten dogs ran in the field in front of them, nowhere where they were supposed to be. "Oh, brother," he said.

"That's what I was thinking," Rex said. "I'm going to *kill* my brother."

DARREN GOT USED to his new routine, and he found a soulmate in Sarena, who hated Halloween as much as he did.

Neither of them dressed up, though Sorrell donned a blonde wig and went to work at the community center as Dolly Parton, and Serendipity apparently wore the same thing every year—a sasquatch outfit.

She didn't lead tour groups on Halloween, but she posed as Big Foot in the woods. She thought it was hilarious, but Darren simply didn't get what was funny about it. He and Sarena wore their jeans and boots and cowboy hats and went to work.

He'd learned how to clean up after himself in the bathroom, after she'd kindly pointed out that they had one sink to share. He'd told her that he and Diana had each had their own sink, and he hadn't even thought about it.

Now, he saw where he left his boots by the back door, and where he hung his jacket and his hat by the front one. He saw evidence of himself on the end tables, in the kitchen, everywhere in the house except for Sorrell's and Serendipity's bedrooms.

As November wore on, Darren couldn't ignore his promptings to call his mother any longer. She hadn't called or texted to invite him for Thanksgiving, because he'd declined since he'd left the Frio area, four years ago. With a pang of regret, he realized she'd given up, and he decided he'd call and find out what his parents were doing.

But first, he needed to know what Sarena's family traditions were. He waited until she came out of the bathroom wearing the silky blue pajamas he sure had grown to like. "I wanted to ask you something," he said.

"All right." She climbed onto the bed but didn't get

beneath the covers. "Go for it. Then I have to go grab something I got in the mail today. I forgot about it until just now."

He looked at her, finding her adorable and soft with her hair down out of its customary ponytail. When she wasn't wearing a hat or a flannel shirt, she was downright breathtaking. He liked the cowgirl version of her too, and she was as strong physically as she was mentally.

"Something serious?" he asked.

"Not for us," she said with a smile. "But I wanted to show it to you and get your opinion."

"Go grab it."

"No, you ask me what you wanted to ask me first."

"Okay." He reached down and stroked Koda, stealing some of the dog's calm energy. He still wouldn't come with Darren first thing in the morning, and if he couldn't get to the fence to see Sarena, she drove him over and dropped him off at Chestnut Ranch.

"It's about Thanksgiving," he said. "What do you and your family do?"

"Sorrell cooks," she said. "My grandmother—my mom's mother—taught her, and she loves it. She should start cooking any day now, and I'd be surprised if she didn't already have the menu planned, with lists made."

"So us going to Frio to visit my parents is probably not something that'll happen this year."

"Oh, Darren, I didn't know you wanted to go visit your parents."

"I didn't either." He looked at her. "I never did tell them about us."

She turned and faced him, crossing her legs underneath her. "I can talk to Sorrell."

"What if I invited my parents up here?"

Surprise rolled across her face. "We've...well, I know you didn't know my dad, but he never hosted anything here at Fox Hollow."

"If you don't want to—"

"I do," she blurted out. "I tried to get Daddy off this ranch more times than I can count. But he'd never go. So we got used to having our own celebrations."

"Why wouldn't he leave the ranch?"

Sarena's expression changed to one with sadness around the edges. "He had a falling-out with his brother, and he only has the one. His parents sided with Uncle Dale, I guess, I don't really know what it was about."

"And that's why it's weird he'd have a clause in the will requiring you to get married." She'd told him that she'd told her cowboys about the stipulation, and how surprised they'd both been. She'd been trying to figure out when the change in the will had been made, and Janelle Stokes was apparently looking into it.

As far as Darren knew, Sarena hadn't heard anything yet.

"Right," Sarena said. "So anyway, since they all live here in Chestnut Springs, he just decided not to leave the ranch anymore."

"How long did he stay confined to Fox Hollow?"

"Oh, years," Sarena said, blowing out her breath. "Probably eighteen by the time he died. Right after my mother—" She cut off suddenly, her eyes going wide.

Darren knew what came next. Right after her mother had died. "Maybe it had nothing to do with Uncle Dale at all," he said quietly.

Sarena shook her head. He'd never seen her shed a tear over her mother—or her accident, or her prosthetic. "I don't—maybe not."

"I didn't want to leave Lantern Hill after Diana died," he said, his mind automatically flowing back to the very first time he'd come back to the ranch and the homestead all by himself. A house had never felt so big and so overwhelming. Just like he could see every surface and room he'd touched here in the farmhouse, the same had been true for Diana in the home she'd started to build with Darren.

"But you did," Sarena said.

"Yeah," Darren said with a sigh. "After the first few days, seeing all the reminders of her was much harder than walking away from the ranch."

"There aren't any reminders of my mother here," Sarena said. "Daddy boxed everything up and got rid of it."

"He threw it out?" Darren looked at her. "Really?"

"What did you do with Diana's things?"

"They're in a storage unit in Hondo," he said instantly. "I couldn't throw anything away, even the ugly Christmas sweater her brother had given her that she hated." He chuckled, quickly sobering as he shook his head. "It doesn't make sense, I know. But I couldn't do it." He shrugged, wondering if he went back to that storage unit now, if he'd be able to comb through Diana's clothes and shoes and jewelry and be able to pick out only the best pieces.

Sarena fell silent, and it took Darren a few minutes to notice. She went mute whenever she was working through something in her mind, and Darren asked, "What's in your head?"

"I'm thinking maybe my parents weren't as happy as I thought they were. Maybe Daddy didn't leave the ranch, because he was...I don't know. He didn't want...I don't know. Maybe he just didn't want to interact with anyone anymore."

Darren nodded. "You think there's something else going on?"

"Why do you retreat from people?" she asked.

"When I'm angry," he said, still stroking Koda. "I like to be alone. When I'm frustrated. When I'm embarrassed." He met her eyes. "He could've been upset about your mom's death."

"Or he could've had a secret," Sarena said. "One that then caused him to put the stipulation in the will."

Darren tried to stay on the same train of thought as her. "So you think he felt guilty for something, so he willed the ranch to Dale...but only if you didn't get married?"

"I have no idea." Sarena sighed and lay down, stretching out and looking up at the ceiling. "I just don't want to think about this anymore. But it really doesn't make sense to will the ranch to Dale. None at all."

"Then we'll figure it out," Darren said. "Can I call my mom in the morning and invite her here for Thanksgiving?"

"I'm sure Sorrell won't mind," Sarena said. "She always makes enough food for at least two dozen people. Theo and Phillip will be here too."

"I'll call in the morning then," he said. "Are you gonna go get that thing?"

"Yes," she said, jumping up from the bed. "We need something lighthearted to talk about."

He smiled as she walked out of the room in the unique gait she had because of her partial foot. She returned a minute later, a single, regularly-sized envelope in her hand. "This came today. Seren usually gets the mail, but I was out by the road today, chasing down a wayward goat, and I grabbed it."

She passed him the envelope, which had Sorrell's name on it. No last name. "You opened your sister's mail? That's a federal offense, you know." He grinned at Sarena, who just rolled her eyes.

"Read it," she said.

"No return address," he said. "There's not even a stamp on it."

"So it doesn't qualify as mail anyway," Sarena said.

Darren glanced at her, and then back to the envelope, which had piqued his interest. He took out a single sheet of paper, which had handwriting on it that clearly belonged to a man. "Dear Sorrell," he read. "I just watched this movie about a girl who writes love letters to all the boys she's ever loved. I decided I could do the same thing, but the thing is, you're the only woman I've ever loved."

He stopped reading, because he felt like he was intruding on an extremely private moment. "Who sent this?" He skipped to the end of the letter, which only filled half of one side of the sheet of paper. "There's no name."

"It's from Theo." Sarena sighed. "He's loved Sorrell for ages."

"Why won't she go out with him?"

"If I got a letter like that, I would," Sarena said. "But Sorrell's...she's really dramatic, right? She has a quick smile, and she's always been a glass-half-full kind of person. But she had a very bad experience with a man, and nothing can change her mind that there are good men out there."

Darren didn't know what to say. "She's nice to me."

"Yeah, and she goes out with people here and there," Sarena said. "Nothing serious. Ever."

"So why can't she go out with Theo a time or two? Keep it casual?"

"Because she likes him too much." Sarena took the letter from him, carefully folding it and putting it back in the envelope. "We need to find a way to get her to go out with him."

"We do?"

Sarena smiled, though her eyes remained serious. "Yes, cowboy," she said. "We do."

"How in the world are we going to do that?" Darren didn't even have the glimmer of an idea. He wasn't a matchmaker; he couldn't even get his own dates before he'd met Sarena sobbing at the back fence.

"She likes quotes," she said. "So you need to start dropping them as little hints about how great cowboys are."

"What are you talking about?"

"I've already found your first one for you," she said, twisting to put the letter in the top drawer of the nightstand beside the bed. She plucked a new slip of paper from it and handed it to him.

"A true cowboy you never have to question their honesty, integrity, or motives," he read. He looked at her, confusion running through him like a river. "I don't get it."

"We start talking about cowboys, and how amazing they are, and you can say little things like that."

"And you think that's going to work?" He shook his head and looked at the quote she'd printed out. "Sorrell's not stupid. She's going to figure out what I'm doing, and then *I* look like the fool."

"No," Sarena said. "This is going to work, I promise." She took the paper from him and dropped it on top of the nightstand this time. "Now, tomorrow morning, you're going to first compliment her on her coffee…"

Sarena kept outlining the planned conversation in her mind, and Darren just let her do it. He liked listening to her talk, and he admired that she cared so much about her sister to spend so much time planning this.

No, he didn't think it would work, because Sorrell wasn't a puppet, and no matter how badly Sarena wanted her to play the part, she didn't have to follow the script.

But Darren held his wife close as they continued to talk into the night, happier than he'd been in a long, long time.

CHAPTER 16

S arena stepped into the back shed, the familiar scent of dirt and old cardboard assaulting her. She'd been sneaking in here for the past few days, calling it a lunch hour as she ate a peanut butter sandwich, drank a bottle of water, and went through everything her sisters had boxed up from her father's room.

She knew what the affairs of the ranch were. When she'd taken over for her father just over five years ago, they'd gone through every piece of paper in the office in the barn. But her conversation with Darren from a week ago wouldn't leave her mind. She had to know why her father wouldn't leave the ranch after Mama's death, and she agreed with Theo and Phillip. There had to be a reason Daddy had put Uncle Dale in the will.

She just hadn't found it yet.

The boxes to her left had been searched and stacked out of the way. She easily had half of the boxes still to go, and a determination unlike anything she'd ever felt before. The only thing she'd felt more passionately about was finding someone who would marry her so Uncle Dale wouldn't get the ranch.

Janelle had given her a date for the will's amendment, but that was all the lawyer had been able to find.

"April twentieth," she muttered to herself as she walked toward the next box she was going to tackle. The date meant nothing to her. Her mother had died in February, twelve years before Daddy had changed the will.

"Why was April so significant?" she wondered. She could barely remember five days ago, let alone five years. And at this point, in another five months, it would've been six years.

She opened the top of the box by slicking through the clear packing tape with the pocketknife she'd brought with her the first day she'd lunched in the shed. Clothes filled it, and she tucked the flaps and moved the box to the searched pile.

She was only interested in papers. Journals. Books. Envelopes. Anything that might have some sort of document in it. She didn't care about her father's clothes or shoes or trinkets—at least not for this project.

Three more boxes of clothing joined the stack, and she hadn't realized how many clothes her father had had. When Darren had moved in, he'd probably had a dozen boxes, only half of which had actually held clothes. Sarena could scarcely think of Darren without smiling, as he'd changed her life in every way possible.

She took a bite of her peanut butter sandwich and opened another box. Bingo. This one contained several bound volumes, as well as file folders bursting with papers. Sarena sat on the chair she'd brought out and started removing things from the box one at a time.

Every book, even novels, got their pages fanned to make sure nothing had been stuck inside. Gradually, her sandwich disappeared and her water got drank as she looked through the box.

"Nothing." Frustration accompanied the word, and for the first time since she'd started this project, she thought she might never find what she was looking for. If she *knew* what she was looking for, that might help.

Her timer hadn't gone off yet, so Sarena repacked the box with the benign books and papers, moved it, and went back for another one.

The next box she opened was different, in that it wasn't the same new, brown ones Sorrell or Seren had obviously gotten from a storage facility. This box was white, and wider, with something written on top in green permanent marker that had been scribbled out.

Because this box was bigger, it had been placed on the bottom of the stack, and she had to squat to reach it. Sarena peered closer at it, her thighs burning the longer she studied the writing. Was it her mother's?

Her memories of her mother had faded considerably over the years, and finally Sarena made out the words *adams family*, all lowercase.

She lifted the top off the box and found what looked like the inner workings of a filing cabinet. Daddy hadn't kept one of those in the farmhouse, at least not to Sarena's knowledge.

There were no books, no journals, nothing bound

together. Only files with loose papers inside them. The first one contained city bills from Chestnut Springs, along with old garbage and recycling schedules, city newsletters outlining events and community classes, and a sticky note taped to the inside front of the folder with the phone numbers for utilities, water emergencies, and how to report a gas leak.

The handwriting belonged to her mother, and Sarena just stared at it. These weren't Daddy's files. These were Mama's.

She hadn't quite found her courage to ask Sorrell or Seren where their father had put their mother's things. She hadn't even thought about them in so long, and Sorrell had been at college when their mother had died. Seren had been a junior in high school, and she'd barely finished out the year.

Sarena herself had been in such a daze, and she literally had no recollection of when her father had cleaned out her mother's belongings. She must've been around, but he could've easily done what she was doing right then—going through things while she'd been out working on the ranch.

She set the Chestnut Springs file aside and reached for another one. This folder held only a couple of pieces of paper and didn't bear a label.

She opened the folder and sucked in a gasp. She knew exactly what this was, because she and Darren had gotten one in the mail a few weeks ago.

A marriage certificate.

And it had her mother's name on it...and Uncle Dale's.

"What in the world?" Sarena couldn't pick it up fast enough. Sure enough, it said Dale Adams as the husband, and they'd been married forty-five years ago.

Sarena's heart raced as fast as her mind did. She'd been born only two years after that. Was Dale her father?

"Please, no," she whispered, feeling frantic and out of control. Her fingers shook as she put the first marriage certificate behind the next piece of paper—which was also a marriage certificate.

Her eyes bounced along the words, skipping over letters and sentiments to find the names, the dates.

Susan Wiggins. Her mother.

William Adams. Her father.

They'd been married the same year Sarena had been born —only seven months before she'd been born.

Relief started to tumble through her, but her heart continued to thrash. "Just because they were married when you were born doesn't mean you're his." Her father and Dale were brothers. She looked like her sisters, but that didn't mean a whole lot. She needed proof—definitive proof—that she belonged to her father.

The folder held nothing else, and Sarena quickly reached for the next file. This one boasted old, acid-ruined pictures of what looked like a wedding. She couldn't make out any of the faces, and the writing on the back had blurred long ago.

Another folder. Another set of papers that took Sarena a moment to identify. "This is Mama's will," she said, finally getting what all the legal jargon meant. She leafed through it one page at a time, and on the third page, another note had been stuck, this time with her father's handwriting on it.

Susan's will—outdated it read. *Where's the most currently executed will?*

Sarena didn't know how to breathe. Several lines in the will, right below the note, had been highlighted in yellow. She could practically see her father with that yellow highlighters, bent over this will, reading and underlining.

The parcel of land deemed Fox Hollow Ranch, which belongs to Susan Wiggins, will pass to her husband upon her death. Susan desires the ranch to stay in the family, as it has been for generations, and encourages her husband to pass the ranch to their oldest daughter upon his death.

Right below that, in tiny, black letters, someone had written *Who's the oldest daughter?*

Sarena let out a cry, her adrenaline kicking in and causing her to stand suddenly. She couldn't read this. She simply couldn't. She'd thought she wanted to know, but she didn't.

But her mother hadn't even named her husband in her will. So did the ranch go to Daddy or to Uncle Dale?

If this wasn't the real will, where was the updated one? What did it say?

Was this why Daddy had put his stipulation in his will? He hadn't passed the ranch to any single one of his daughters. He'd simply said it would go to *all* of them, provided *one* of them got married first.

Sarena couldn't think inside the shed, and she burst out of the doors, sucking at the air. She bent over, bracing herself against her knees as she tried to breathe in and out normally. Her mind malfunctioned, and her body took over. Her heart beat, because it always did. Her lungs expanded, because that was their job.

"Sarena?"

She looked up at the male voice, but it took her eyes several seconds to focus on Theo.

"Are you okay?" He came toward her, and Sarena couldn't get her voice to work. Theo put his arm through hers and added, "Come sit down." He got her into the house and to the table, where she sat.

Before she knew it, he'd put a bottle of water in front of her and commanded her to drink while he opened the window to "let in some fresh air." Sarena took a sip, some of her senses coming back to her as the cool air from outside washed across her face.

"What's going on?"

She couldn't get her thoughts to line up, so she just shook her head. "I'm okay."

"Is it something with Darren?"

"No," she said. "He just said something the other night that reinforced what you and Phillip had said about my dad and Dale, and I started looking through some of his boxes."

"Out in the shed?"

"Yeah."

"What did you find?"

"I don't really know yet," she said, squaring her shoulders. "So I can't say anything yet." She narrowed her eyes at him. "And you can't tell Sorrell."

"Like that's even a possibility," he said. "She won't even text me back."

"What?" Sarena asked, uncapping her bottle for another drink. "She told me she was talking to you. Darren and I have been working on her from here at the farmhouse."

"She—what? Working on her?" He glared at her. "What does that mean?"

Sarena's heart was going to need electrical jolts to keep it beating normally. "Just...you know. I'm encouraging her to date again, and specifically to go out with you."

"You have got to be kidding me."

"I thought you wanted her to go out with you."

"I do, but not because you and your fake-husband conned her into it."

"We didn't *con* her," Sarena said, her pulse rapid-firing now for another reason. "And listen, I didn't tell you about Darren so you could throw it back in my face."

"Yeah, well, I haven't said a word to you about Sorrell at all."

The fight left Sarena, and she sagged back against her chair. "I know. I'm sorry. It's just...you two would be *perfect* for each other, and she just needs a nudge."

"Like you and Darren," he said.

Sarena just shrugged, because she didn't want to go all the way to perfect yet. "The will was a nudge, I suppose."

"You like him, right?"

"I mean, I guess," she said, not really wanting to talk about her feelings with her hired cowboy, though she and Theo were friends. "We're still working through some things."

"You gonna stay married?"

"Probably not," she said, needing to move this conversation onto something else. "Listen—"

The back door crashed into the wall near Sarena. "We're

not going to stay married?" Darren stood there, his chest heaving. "And what do you mean you *guess* you like me?"

An electrical storm entered the farmhouse with him, and Sarena felt frozen to the chair where she sat.

"See you later," Theo said, making a hasty escape while Darren glared at her.

"If this is not real, what is it?" He gestured between the two of them. "It feels real to me."

"It's real to me too," she said.

"I don't play games with my heart, and certainly not with the sanctity of marriage, Sarena. If this is a joke to you, I'm done. I was willing to do it so you could keep Fox Hollow. But you don't get to have it both ways."

"Did you hear what I said? I said it was real to me too." She stood up, her emotions all over the place.

"Sure," he said. "All right. Fine."

"What are you even doing here?"

"You were supposed to meet me at the back fence for lunch," he said. "You didn't show up, and I was worried about you." His fingers clenched into fists, and Sarena could practically see his thoughts streaming through his head.

She'd never seen Darren this angry before.

"I'll be home late," he said. "Cards with the Chestnut cowboys tonight." He spun and headed right back out the door, nothing bothering to close it behind him.

"Darren," she called after him. When she reached the door, he had one hand up in the air in a farewell wave and he was already moving down the steps from the deck. He didn't look back, not even once.

———

Chapter 17

Brian Gray really needed to get back to the ranch, or someone would notice he'd snuck away. He couldn't force himself to do it yet, though.

"Anyway," Serendipity said. "I've talked your ear off enough about the hiking trail to the springs."

"We should go," he said, though he'd said it before. He tensed, waiting for Serendipity to contradict him.

"Yeah, but not until spring," she said, which was at least a new excuse for not wanting to be seen with him in public. He understood why; at least he'd tried to. "I have to go," she said, sitting up and starting to scoot to the end of the tailgate. "Thanks for bringing that roast beef sandwich. It's my favorite."

She threw him a flirty smile over her shoulder and jumped down to the ground. Brian sighed as he stood up and launched himself over the side of the truck, landing neatly on his feet though a shock went through his cowboy boots and up his legs.

He didn't hug her good-bye, and they were still miles from kissing. He'd been sneaking off the ranch at quitting time and they'd been holding hands, sharing dinner, and swapping ranch stories—and nature guide stories—since Darren had moved in with Sarena.

Brian had taken Darren a couple of new dog bowls as a moving present, and Serendipity had answered the door. He'd seen her at the wedding, but he truly been smitten with one look at her pretty face when she'd opened that door. He'd somehow gotten her number before he left the property.

Of course, she'd practically chased him down the dirt road to give it to him. They'd been seeing each other in the evenings since, and he sure did like texting her too.

She wasn't super keen on doing anything more than that, though, and she'd declined his invitation to drive her to town and pay for her dinner. Or pick her up from the Ranger station where she worked and take her somewhere to eat. So he brought food from town to the ranch, where he parked in a grove of trees only fifty feet from the highway. They talked. They ate. They held hands.

Then Serendipity slipped away from him like smoke.

Brian stuffed his frustration down into his stomach, where he'd eaten too much roast beef. He wanted to take a shower and go to bed, but it was Thursday, and that meant all the boys would be coming over to play cards.

He arrived back to the cabin he shared with Tomas at the same time Aaron opened the front door of the house next door. Darren had used to live there, but Aaron had moved in when he'd moved out. Brian couldn't lie and say he wasn't happy about the new living arrangements. It had been cramped with three of them in one cabin, despite the extra square footage it had over Aaron's smaller cabin.

"You're just getting back?" Aaron called as he crossed the yellowing grass between the two cabins.

"Yeah," Brian said, and that was all. He found that he didn't need to offer a reason unless someone asked. And Aaron rarely did. Tomas either. So he didn't have to lie to them if he said nothing.

"Darren said he's gonna be a little late," Aaron said. "Did you get his text?"

"Haven't checked," Brian said. "If he's going to be late, I have time to shower." They went up the steps together, and Brian opened the door to the cabin. Tomas stood at the back of the house, in the kitchen, wearing a pair of oven mitts.

"Pizza's out," he said. "Darren's going to be late."

"Yeah," Brian said. "Aaron just told me. I'm going to hop in the shower real quick. Be right back." He went down the short hall and into the bathroom he shared with Tomas. As a career cowboy, he knew how to shower in less than five minutes, as he sometimes had to bathe two or three times each day.

So only ten minutes later, clean and deodorized, Brian padded back into the kitchen wearing a pair of shorts and a T-shirt and ready to pretend like he was starving. He put two pieces of pizza on a plate and picked up a piece of garlic bread for good measure.

It actually tasted like manna from heaven in his mouth, and by the time he finished the delicious bread, his stomach was begging him not to eat any more. Thankfully, Darren walked in, and Brian handed him the plate of pizza. "Here you go."

Darren took it, the displeasure on his face plain to see. "This is for me?"

"That's right." Brian looked at Tomas and Aaron, both of whom had their eyes glued to Darren. "What's goin' on with you?"

"Nothing," Darren said, but the man's whole countenance was as dark as midnight. He took the pizza over to the table and sat in his normal seat. Brian didn't see another choice for him, so he grabbed a soda and joined his friends.

Tomas shuffled the cards, a wide grin on his face. "Who's ready to lose tonight?"

Darren was, that was for sure. The man had decent luck with cards, but not when he wasn't focused. Brian's brain felt a bit fuzzy too, and he wished he could just sink onto the couch and put something mindless on the TV. Then he could stare while he daydreamed about Serendipity and if she'd ever let him kiss her.

"Get your cookies, boys," Aaron said, passing around the night's substitute for poker chips. Chips Ahoy. Brian took the ten they all got, and Tomas started throwing cards out.

"The game is five-card draw," he said. "Put in your ante."

Brian's heart wasn't in the game, and he glanced at Darren, who hadn't even taken cookies yet. He'd known him since Darren had come to Chestnut Ranch. Brian wasn't the oldest cowboy there, but he'd been at Chestnut longer than any of the other three at the table with him. And he still felt like he only knew the fringes of Darren Dumond. The surface stuff. The things everyone knew about Darren.

"How's Sarena?" he asked, deciding to be daring and put the question out there.

Darren actually growled and tossed in a cookie with the words, "Two." He put two cards down on the table, and Tomas traded them for a couple of others.

"That good, huh?" Aaron asked. "I thought marriage was supposed to be bliss for at least the first year."

"No," Tomas said. "The first year is the hardest. That's what I read."

"Oh, well, I've never been married, so I wouldn't know." Aaron slid three cards to Tomas, who replaced them.

Brian kept his mouth shut. He'd been married, and it had been a disaster. He hadn't even made it a year, so he definitely agreed with Tomas. He switched out one card and didn't get what he needed to win the hand. Instead of losing cookies, he folded and let the others play out the hand.

The conversation stalled, and Brian didn't like the silence. They'd never had a problem keeping things lively during their card nights, but Darren had never shown up with such a storm in his soul either.

"Just tell us what's going on," Brian finally said. He only had two cookies left anyway, and his patience had run out twenty minutes ago.

"I'm fine," Darren said. "I am tired though, so I best be getting back to Fox Hollow." He stood up and took his plate with him into the kitchen. That sentence had been the longest he'd spoken that night.

Brian wanted to follow him out the back door and ask him what was really going on, but the way Darren cast him a pointed look said he better not.

So he'd text him. Brian needed to start getting outside his fences too, and he might as well start with Darren. *If you need something, let me know,* he typed out and sent. *I've been married before, and it can be real tough sometimes.*

He wasn't revealing any secrets; the other boys knew he'd been married before. They didn't know his marriage had only lasted three months, because they'd never asked. Brian was the king of keeping things to himself unless someone asked.

It was why he liked Serendipity so much. She asked a ton of questions, as if she really wanted to get to know him. And he liked telling her the answers to whatever she asked.

Darren didn't answer, which really solidified for Brian that something was wrong. He thanked the others for the game, helped Tomas clean up, and went down the hall to his bedroom. Finally alone with more than a few seconds to think, he sent a quick text to Serendipity.

Maybe we could drive to Austin on Friday night. There's a great pizza place there.

She'd say no. A long drive on a Friday night? She'd have to explain something to her sisters. But at least no one from Chestnut Springs would spot them in Austin.

She didn't answer either, and Brian went to bed, wondering if his phone had malfunctioned on him. All seemed okay with it. The bottom line was no one was texting him back.

Story of my life, he thought as he switched off the lamp and stared up in to the darkness. He kept his eyes open for as long as he could without blinking, to the point that they teared up.

Then he closed his eyes and said, "Lord, I'd sure like to go out properly with Serendipity Adams. Can You help me with that, please?"

CHAPTER 18

Serendipity Adams emerged from the hallway that led from the front door of the farmhouse and knew something was wrong. Number one, Sarena stood in the kitchen, a bowl on the counter in front of her and a cookbook open next to her.

"This isn't good," she muttered to herself. "Where's Sorrell?" she asked louder. "I thought she was making the hummus and pitas tonight." Not that Serendipity cared. Brian had brought her the beefiest roast beef sandwich in the county, and she wasn't anywhere near hungry.

She also absolutely could not tell her sisters about Brian. Serendipity didn't even know what their relationship was, and Sarena would ask a million questions. Sorrell would be horrified and hurt, and Serendipity couldn't do that to her sister.

If only Sorrell could get past what Ethan had done to her. Then they could all move on. As it was, Serendipity felt stuck behind a tall wall of plastic she could neither scale nor break down.

"She got called into a last-minute meeting," Sarena said, throwing what looked like a lot of salt to Serendipity into the bowl in front of her. "So I'm making meatballs. She didn't say anything about hummus."

Her sister still hadn't looked at her, and Serendipity was no stranger to reading a room. "What's wrong?"

"Nothing," Sarena said. "Why should something be wrong?" She fixed a hard stare at Serendipity, challenging her to call things how she saw them.

Seren lifted her chin. "Well, you don't cook for one," she said. "And this place feels like someone hooked a vacuum to it and sucked out all the air for another."

Sarena rolled her eyes, igniting Seren's irritation. "I'm not hungry," she said. "I'm going to go read in bed." She left the kitchen despite Sarena muttering something under her breath. How she hated that. If Seren had something to say, she just said it. Sarena was much more passive-aggressive with all the muttering.

Seren had called her on it a couple of times in the past, but she didn't have the energy tonight. Her sister was dealing with a lot—a new husband, a new role around the ranch, and who knew what else. Seren could give her a pass this one time.

She knew she needed them from time to time, and she appreciated it when Sarena gave her the benefit of the doubt. Not only that, but Sarena worked like a dog around the ranch. She always had, even when she'd been seriously injured. She was the one who took care of everything, and Seren reminded herself that without Sarena's sacrifice by marrying Darren, they wouldn't have the ranch for much longer.

It was those thoughts that drove her back out to the kitchen, where Sarena scooped up another ball of meat and practically threw it into the baking dish. "It's obvious you're upset," Seren said.

"Yes." Sarena spooned more meat into her hands and started rolling.

"About what?"

"So many things." She shot a glance in Seren's direction. "When you and Sorrell went through Daddy's things, did you look at any of them?"

"Not really," Seren said, sitting at the island where her sister worked. "If there was something obviously dirty or ruined, we threw it away."

"Like, his clothes and stuff."

"Yeah, and the golf clubs he used to beat the ground with," Seren said. "Stuff like that."

"But you didn't go through any of his files or anything."

"No. We boxed them up and cleaned them out." She watched Sarena, as it was clear her sister had something on her mind. "Why?"

"No reason."

"You're such a bad liar," Seren said, adding a laugh to the end of it so as to not further enrage Sarena. "Just tell me."

"Do you know what Mama's will said?" Sarena asked instead.

"I have no idea." Seren's defenses went right up, and she wasn't even sure why. "I was seventeen when she died."

"Right." Sarena finished with the meatballs and turned to get the sauce off the stove. She poured that all over the meatballs and slid the baking dish into the oven.

"Why do you need her will?" Seren asked.

"Because," Sarena said. "The one I found is outdated, and I want to see the one that was executed."

Seren frowned, confusion riddling her mind. "But why?"

"Because it's important," Sarena said, reaching for a disinfectant wipe and swiping at the countertop. "Doesn't it seem weird to you that Daddy said one of us had to get married or the ranch would go to Uncle Dale? I mean, on what planet does that make any sense?"

"It doesn't make sense," Seren agreed.

"Right, so I need to know why Daddy did that. And I think it has something to do with Mama."

"What would it have to do with her?" Seren wished Sarena would stop with the wiping and cleaning. Her energy was made of nerves, and it was driving Seren up the wall. "And I can help."

That got Sarena to stop. "Could you?"

"Sure. Point me in the right direction, and I'll help." Just because Seren didn't have a rancher's blood in her veins didn't mean she couldn't contribute. For a long time, that was how Daddy and Sarena had made her feel, but she had more confidence now.

"Okay," Sarena said. "This weekend, we'll go through the files in the shed." She looked like she might cry. "I don't think I can do it alone anymore." Her bottom lip trembled, and Seren hurried around the island to take Sarena into a hug.

"You don't have to do anything alone," she said. "You have me and Sorrell to help. And now your handsome husband."

Sarena only cried harder, and Seren didn't understand it. She knew Darren hadn't moved across the hall to Daddy's room, which meant he and Sarena were sleeping in the same room. Showering in the same bathroom. They seemed to get along so well, but something was seriously wrong tonight.

"What's going on?" Serendipity begged, stepping back and holding her sister by the shoulders. That was one good thing about being the tallest sister. "You can tell me."

"Oh, I got all stressed out going through files this afternoon, and then Theo found me, and he started asking all these questions about Darren too, and he overheard me say some things—but they were out of context. Of course the marriage is real for me too." She sucked in a breath, her eyes going wide.

Serendipity searched Sarena's face. "You're in love with him." She wasn't asking a real question, because she could see it in the anguish of her sister's eyes.

Sarena nodded, and Serendipity smiled. The front door opened, and Sorrell sang out, "Okay, I'm home, my lovely sisters."

They turned toward her as she came down the hall, and Seren had no idea what sight Sorrell saw. But she froze when she finally stepped into the back of the house. "What's happening?" She looked from Sarena to Serendipity to some point behind both of them. "Who tried to make dinner in that oven? It has cheese burnt all over the bottom of it."

Serendipity's next breath tasted like smoke, and she spun toward the oven to find thick, gray smoke billowing out of the vents. She didn't take a single step toward it, though, because Sorrell would take care of it.

Sure enough, the middle sister who'd gotten all the organizational and culinary genes swept past them and removed the baking dish and flipped off the oven, seemingly in less time than it took to inhale.

"Well," she said. "It seems like a real party here tonight." They both watched as Sarena wiped her eyes, clearing away the evidence of her crying.

"Let's go to dinner," Serendipity said, though her stomach cramped at the thought. "Sarena's got some stories to tell."

Serendipity did too, but she had a hunch Sarena's tales would trump hers—and right now, that was just fine. She was perfectly okay with keeping Brian Gray a secret a little longer.

CHAPTER 19

Darren left the cabin, then the ranch, his mood no better now than it had been a couple of hours ago. To think, he'd jumped the fence at Fox Hollow just after lunch, worried about Sarena.

The thought made him scoff, and he hated the darkness inside him. He'd been getting rid of it so well, too.

His insecurities twisted and turned, and Darren couldn't press against the self-loathing hard enough. It ran through him, breaking through the barriers he'd put in place in the past. No amount of self-talk was going to save him this time.

He drove into town and eased his truck down Main Street, the quaint square passing by on his left as shop after shop lit the sky on his right. With Thanksgiving next week, and Christmas after that, the city had already put up their holiday decorations. Toy soldiers and Christmas trees waved to him from the lampposts, and Darren made turns without making conscious decisions.

Before he knew it, he'd left the town he'd grown to love in his rear-view mirror and only had the dark Hill Country in front of him. The roads beyond the tiny towns that dotted this part of Texas dipped and rose, twisted and turned. He loved them, but he'd grown up driving them. To him, there was nothing better than driving down a dark road, his headlights the only thing brightening the landscape in front of him as he carved a tunnel through the trees.

So many trees in the Texas Hill Country, and Darren wished he could be like them. Strong. Resilient. Immovable.

By the time he made his way back to Fox Hollow, he felt sure Sarena would be asleep. He'd be cursing himself in the morning, which was only a few hours away at this point. As he went slowly down the dirt lane that led to the farmhouse, his tires crunching over the dirt and rocks, he considered simply sleeping in his truck.

He wasn't going to go crawling back to Sarena's bed, that was for dang sure. Another dose of idiocy shot through him, and he killed the headlights the moment the farmhouse came into view. He continued to his normal parking spot in front of the house and looked through the windshield to the porch.

The motion sensor light hadn't activated, and Darren breathed a sigh of relief. If he tried going in, though, that bright light would fill the area around the front of the house. Yes, sleeping in the truck seemed like his best option. He had a charger for his phone, and the alarm would go off in six hours.

Before he could move, and still completely unsure about what to do, the light flooded the porch and spilled out onto the little patch of grass in front of the house.

Darren stared as Sarena moved along the length of the porch and curled her hand around the pillar that guarded the steps leading down to the front sidewalk.

"Can't leave now," he muttered to himself. He couldn't sleep in the truck either. So he sighed as he unbuckled his seat belt and got out of the vehicle. The squeal of the door as he slammed it made him cringe. Everything was far too quiet out here, and he decided to mimic it.

Sarena was the one who needed to talk anyway. Darren had already spectacularly embarrassed himself in front of her —and Theo.

He stuck his hands in his pockets as he approached her, stalling a healthy distance from the bottom of the steps, which she'd come down.

"Hey," she said, clearly nervous.

He nodded at her, glad he literally wore his cowboy hat day and night. Then he could keep it tilted low enough for him to see her face but keep his in mostly shadows.

"You're mad," she said. "I'm—you weren't supposed to hear all that stuff."

Instant fury roared through him, but he clenched his teeth together.

"None of it was true," she said. "I said it as a defense mechanism against Theo."

"Why?" Darren growled. "You got a thing for Theo?"

Her mouth dropped open, and she blinked at him. "That was a joke, right?"

"You tell me."

She took a step toward him, fire practically leaping from

her eyes. "Of course I don't have a thing for Theo. I'm in love with *you*." She gestured wildly, indicating everything around her. "You've just waltzed into my life, changing everything, and you're just...amazing, and I didn't want to tell my *employee* any of that." Her chest heaved, and she marched in his direction now, stopping only two steps short of running straight into him.

"I'd already told him and Phillip that we'd gotten married to save the ranch, and I didn't feel the need to get into my *deep, personal* feelings with Theo." She reached out and pushed one palm against his chest. "And you're just...dense if you don't know how I really feel about you, despite what you might've overheard me say to someone."

Darren fell back a step from the push, but mostly from her tongue-lashing. She wasn't afraid to stand up for herself, that was for sure.

"That's it," she said. "That's all I've got, Darren. If it's not good enough, so be it." She folded her arms and glared at him. "I love you. Of course I do. You think I'm letting every man with a sexy hat into my bedroom?" She shook her head and looked away, a sniffle following the statement. She swiped at her eyes.

"I can't say anything else. You decide what you want to do." She looked back at him again, her eyes glassy and hard. "No, I do have one more thing to say. I'm sorry. I don't think I've said that yet, and I need to. I'm sorry, Darren."

His automatic response was to repeat it back to her, but he took a moment to examine himself. Did he want to apologize to her?

Yes.

Did he need to?

Yes.

He had stormed out of the farmhouse and away from her, despite her calling after him. He'd just been so angry, and he'd needed time to cool down.

"I'm sorry too," he said, breaking the silence between them.

"Kiss me?" she asked, her voice pitching up.

Darren didn't want to witness her crying, and his heart squeezed at the anguish he caught in her eyes as he swept toward her. He gathered her right into his arms, murmuring, "I'm sorry, Sarena. I just needed a few minutes to think through some things."

"You've been gone for hours," she whispered. She clung to him as if she needed him to stand, and Darren hadn't been this needed in such a long time. He loved it. He craved this level of need from another human being.

"I know," he said. "I'm sorry."

"The card game ended a long time ago."

"I just drove around."

"I didn't think you were coming back." Sarena buried her face in his neck and Darren wanted to hold onto this moment forever.

"I came back," Darren said, pulllng back and lowering his head so he could do what she'd asked him to do—kiss her.

She shivered in his arms, and he didn't take as long as he wanted. Instead, he secured her hand in his and went inside with her, all the way down the hall to their bedroom.

He changed and climbed into bed with her, where she snuggled right into his chest and held him like she never wanted to let him go.

Darren finally relaxed, though his mind continued to whisper some negative things. Thankfully, he was so tired, and Sarena was so warm, that he fell asleep quickly.

THE NEXT MORNING, he slept through his alarm and stayed in bed with Sarena until long after they usually got up. He'd texted Seth to say he wasn't feeling well, something that had never kept him from his work on the ranch in the past.

But this was different than a cough or a sore throat. This was a mental and emotional exhaustion that Darren needed a day to remedy.

"I've been going through some boxes in the shed," Sarena said once they'd finally made it down the hall to the kitchen.

"Yeah?" Darren took a bite of his toast while she stirred cream into her coffee.

She nodded, studied the dark liquid like it held secrets she needed to know. "Want to help me this weekend?"

"I'm gonna have to work now," he said. "I could probably help on Sunday afternoon."

"Okay." She looked up at him and smiled, and Darren gazed at her beauty. She wore a hint of hauntedness in her eyes, which only made her even more attractive to him.

"Want to tell me about it?" he asked.

She drew in a deep breath, blew it out, and took a sip of

her coffee. "Basically, I wanted to find the reason Daddy put the marriage stipulation in his will. So I started digging through the boxes that had come from his room."

He simply watched her, somewhat able to see her gather her courage and her words before she continued.

"I found my mother's will. She owned the ranch, you see. It wasn't my father's land. It was my mother's. She wanted to keep it in the family, and she left it to her husband. Problem is, she was married to both Uncle Dale and Daddy."

"You're kidding," Darren said.

"I wish." She gave a sarcastic scoff and pushed her coffee away. She never ate much in the morning. "She married Uncle Dale first. It didn't last long, though I don't know how long exactly. I was born only seven months after she and Daddy got married."

Darren's toast had been forgotten and sat on his plate, getting cold. "So...what does that mean?"

Sarena shrugged, as if she hadn't thought this through to several different endings. But Darren knew she had. If there was someone who thought as much as he did, it was Sarena.

"The will said that 'her husband,' should pass the ranch on to the oldest daughter."

"So that's you."

"If it's even Daddy's to give me," she said. "She didn't name who the husband was. It could be Uncle Dale, and I... could be his daughter."

Darren felt like someone had filled his chest cavity with ice. "Sarena," he said, but he couldn't come up with anything else.

"That's about how I felt," she said. "I burst out of the shed and that's when Theo found me. Bent over, hyperventilating, I think." She frowned and reached down to adjust something with her foot. "He brought me inside, made me drink something, and then he started asking me questions. I told him a few things I'd found in the shed."

"You must really trust Theo." Darren wasn't jealous exactly. He wasn't sure what monster was currently clawing through his lungs.

"I do," Sarena said. "He's worked here forever, and he knew Daddy as well as I did. He agrees with me that Daddy would've never given the ranch to Uncle Dale."

Darren connected the dots. "Unless it was Uncle Dale's to begin with."

"Per Mama's will."

"Bright stars," Darren said, shaking his head. "So what now?"

"Now, I need to find the official will that was executed. And I need to figure out who my father was." She shook her head. "Is. Who he *is*." Her eyes met Darren's, and he saw panic and fear there. "What if Uncle Dale is my dad? Losing Daddy was the hardest thing I've ever done. This will be so much harder."

A single tear slithered down her cheek, and she made no effort to wipe it away this time.

Darren got up and knelt in front of her, taking her face in both of his hands. "I'm going to tell you something Diana told me once."

Sarena looked at him earnestly, the moment between them so sweet.

"She said that a family is something you choose, not something you're born into," he said. "So I choose you, and you choose me, and we're a family. And we choose Sorrell and Serendipity. And Theo and Phillip. And Seth, Russ, Travis, Rex, and Griffin. They're our family."

Sarena nodded, holding onto her tears bravely before she closed her eyes and let them fall down her face. He held her close and let her wet his shoulder with them as she cried, his heart breaking and healing over and over again until she quieted.

"I love you," he whispered. "Okay, Sarena? I'll always choose you."

She pressed her forehead to his and nodded. "And I love you."

CHAPTER 20

Sarena didn't make a solo trip to the shed to dig through files again. With Darren's help, she did her chores around the ranch on Friday afternoon. Things between them were different now, she knew that. She could feel it.

Their relationship had survived a very hard thing, and she thanked the Lord that Darren had a forgiving heart as she swept out stalls and fed chickens. She added the fact that she'd been able to speak boldly to him in the front yard to her gratitude prayer as she moved over to the pigs to give them their evening meal.

She caught Theo's eye a couple of times, but she didn't speak to him. A flash of irritation moved through her, because Sorrell had lied to her about talking to him. After they'd cleared the farmhouse of the smoke from the oven last night, Sarena had dominated the conversation as she told them about the argument with Darren, and then everything she'd found in the barn.

They'd agreed to help her tomorrow afternoon, and Darren would be there on Sunday.

Buoyed by the support of her family, Sarena managed to arrive back at the farmhouse in a decent mood. Sorrell stood at the island, bent over a cookbook, several bowls on the counter beside her.

She lifted her eyes to Sarena's as she entered and took off her boots with a sigh of relief.

"So?" Sorrell asked. "How did it go with Darren? I didn't see either of you this morning, but his truck was here."

"Darren and I are fine," Sarena said, indecision raging through her. "Sorrell, why won't you go out with Theo?"

Sorrell clearly hadn't been expecting that question, though Sarena had asked it before. The surprise vanished from her face as quickly as it had come. "Because."

"Because why?"

"You know why."

"*He* doesn't know why," Sarena said. "And I'm not sure I do either. It's been twelve years since Ethan."

Sorrell hissed, but Sarena didn't care. She stood up. "Twelve years, Sorrell. It's time to let it go."

"I have let it go," Sorrell said, lifting her chin though she looked back at the cook book. "It's not because of Ethan that I won't go out with Theo."

"You go out with other men," Sarena said.

"I know."

Sarena sat at the bar, realizing Sorrell was making her

favorite food—pork chili with sweet potato boats. "Tell me why you can't go out with him if you're over Ethan."

"Ethan doesn't get to define me anymore," Sorrell said. "Though I don't really think I'm worth—though I'm not really the marrying type."

Sarena heard what Sorrell was about to say, and she hated that her sister didn't see herself as the most beautiful, kind, *worthy* woman in the world. "Yes, you are."

"You always said you wouldn't get married," Sorrell said.

"And I was stupid," Sarena said. "Being married is amazing."

Sorrell met her eyes again, genuine interest in her expression. "Is it really?"

"Yes." Sarena smiled, because she felt the truth of what she'd said all the way down in her soul. "When you can see the man you love every day? Amazing. And you can kiss him, and text him, and know he's going to be there even if you aren't wearing makeup. Or even if you're a mess, crying about something he might think is stupid. It's wonderful." Sarena's emotions surged, and she didn't try to hide them from Sorrell. "It's beautiful to feel loved, and be loved, and to be able to give love back to him. It's...just amazing. Life-changing."

Darren *had* changed her life when he'd taken her to be his wife.

"That's beautiful," Sorrell whispered.

"You could have this with Theo," Sarena said, almost urgently. "He already loves you, Sorrell. And I know you like him."

"And that's precisely why I can't go out with him," she

said, sniffling. "If I go out with Theo, Sarena, I know there's no way to keep it casual. And I only do casual."

"But maybe with him, you won't have to worry about him squeezing the life out of your heart. Maybe he'll breathe life into it."

"It's a beautiful dream," Sorrell said, smiling through her tears. "But it's just that—a dream."

The front door opened, and Seren's footsteps walked in. Sorrell sniffed and spun away from the hallway while their sister came down it, wiping at her eyes before she opened the fridge and bent down to peer inside it.

Sarena's heart hurt for Sorrell, but she couldn't make her change her mind. She knew that much, at least. To give Sorrell another few seconds, she turned toward their younger sister and said, "How was the hiking today?"

* * *

"Nothing in this one," Seren said the next afternoon. The three of them in the shed definitely made for less room, but they'd gone through a lot more boxes.

"It has to be here," Sarena said, eyeing the last six boxes. "Surely Daddy has a copy of the fully executed will."

"Maybe Janelle did it?" Sorrell suggested.

"She's barely older than me," Sarena said. "There's no way she could've done it."

"Was there a firm on the other will?" Seren asked, reaching for the few things they'd found they wanted to keep out of the boxes. Sorrell picked up another box and started cutting through the tape.

"Lincoln and Forke," Seren said. "I've never heard of them."

"They might be out of business," Sarena said.

"Guys," Sorrell said, and Sarena's heart leapt to the back of her throat. She quickly stepped to Sorrell's side, a sense of vertigo making the whole shed spin. She tried to focus as she looked down into the box.

"Lots of files," Sorrell said.

"Every paper has to be examined," Sarena said. "We're looking for anything to do with the ranch, with Mama's death, marriages, birth certificates would be great."

"We have our birth certificates," Seren said.

"They're reissued," Sarena said. "I got mine out last night. It was reissued after Mama died."

The three sisters looked at one another, and the tension in the shed skyrocketed to a new level.

"Okay." She drew a deep breath and reached into the box, extracting one folder of information. "Here we go."

She set the folder on a stack of boxes they'd made so they could easily see what they needed to. Upon opening it, she found old, weathered newspaper clippings. "Headlines," she said, searching for the dates. "This looks like from the day you were born, Seren."

Sure enough, the folder contained scrapbookable items, like the clippings, a few report cards from elementary school, Sorrell's handprint clearly done in preschool, the tags from the hospital that nurses put around baby's ankles, and the like.

Sarena picked up one of the pink bracelets that had been cut and studied it. Her name was there, as was her mother's. That was all. The others were the same, so there was nothing identifying the father there.

Sorrell laid out the next folder, opening it with a look of worry in her eyes. Sarena closed the folder with the memorabilia in it, startled when Sorrell gasped. "It's our birth certificates."

"Why did Daddy get new ones if he had these?" Seren said, crowding in on Sarena's other side.

"Maybe he didn't know," she said, gingerly picking up the grayish piece of paper. "This one's mine." Her name sat there. The right birthday. "It has Daddy's name on it." Relief blipped through her, but she knew it wasn't concrete proof. Mama and Daddy could've put his name on it because they were married.

She needed proof.

She'd looked up DNA kits last night, and she'd almost ordered one.

Seren looked at her birth certificate, and so did Sorrell. Right below that sat Mama's will.

"This is it," Sarena said, a level of adrenaline pumping through her she didn't know how to contain. "It's on page two."

Sorrell turned the page, and more of that yellow highlighter sat there. "Read it," she said, shifting out of the way. "I can't."

Sarena took her spot in front of the folder, her eyes scanning the words, hardly able to hold onto them at all. "The parcel of land deemed Fox Hollow Ranch, which belongs to Susan Wiggins, will pass to her husband, William Adams, upon her death. Susan desires the ranch to stay in the family, as it has been for generations, and encourages her husband to pass the ranch to their oldest daughter upon his death."

She looked up. "It has Daddy's name in it now. So we know that Mama gave the ranch to him."

"It still doesn't say who the oldest daughter it," Seren said, her eyes still on the will. "It says their oldest daughter. If it's not you..." She met Sarena's eye, and they both looked at Sorrell.

"I don't want the ranch," she said. "It's Sarena's. She married Darren."

"Okay, don't panic," Sarena said, though her own pulse seemed to be galloping through her chest. "Obviously, we still don't know anything, other than Mama made sure the ranch went to Daddy, and not Uncle Dale."

Her resolve to make sure Uncle Dale never got his greedy hands on Fox Hollow doubled. "So now we just need to figure out who my father is."

"How can you be so calm about this?" Sorrell asked, her voice pitching up. "I'd be going crazy. I *am* going crazy, and it's not even me."

"And why Daddy put in the stipulation only five years ago," Seren said, both of them ignoring Sorrell's outburst.

"I'm going to bake some brownies," Sorrell said, practically crashing through the door and letting in the sunshine.

Sarena went to close the door behind her, returning to

Seren with, "This was too much for her. I shouldn't have asked her to help."

"She'll be fine," Seren said. "She's just being dramatic."

"At least we'll get brownies out of it," Sarena said. The two of them laughed together, and a bit of the tension in Sarena's shoulders loosened.

"Okay," Seren said. "Oh, here's another will." She picked it up, her eyes moving back and forth rapidly. "It's Daddy's."

"Does it have the marriage stipulation?"

"Looking..." Seren read and flipped a page. Sarena couldn't peer over her sister's shoulder so she leafed through the other documents in the folder. Two titles to trucks her father had bought over the years. The land deed for the ranch.

She shook her head as she set those very important items on the shelf with the other things they'd rescued from this hoard. She wanted to frame the land deed for the ranch, and put it in the office in the barn. That was where it should go, so everyone could see they owned this place.

She set the right will on the shelf too, and added the three original birth certificates to the pile before Seren even moved.

"This one doesn't have anything about any of us having to get married," Seren said. "It's dated only two weeks after Mama died, and it does name you as the inheritor of the ranch." She handed the papers to Sarena, who wasn't sure she had the energy to read them tonight.

"So this must be the one Daddy had changed," Sarena said. "And I have that copy in the house, so we can compare them." She put the will on the shelf too.

"We still don't know *why*," Seren said, diving into the box again to get another file. "Oh, my."

"What?" Sarena did peer over Seren's shoulder this time, but she wasn't sure what she was looking at.

"It's a paternity test," Seren whispered. "Look." She pointed to the top left line. Their father's name sat there. To the right, a line labeled *Paternity* said it all.

"It has been tested and found to show that William Cecil Adams shares the genetic indicators one would expect to see as a contributor to Sarena Susan Adams' genetic profile. This concludes that William Cecil Adams is the biological father of Sarena Susan Adams." Seren lifted her eyes to Sarena's, both of them as wide and round as dinner plates.

Sarena's lungs burned, and she finally allowed them to take a breath. She took the paper from her sister and left the barn, needing to see it and read it for herself under a brighter light. She stood in the sunshine and read silently the same thing Seren had just said out loud.

She closed her eyes and tipped her head toward the sky. "Thank you, Lord. Thank you, thank you, thank you."

CHAPTER 21

Darren hurried back to the farmhouse after doing the morning chores at Chestnut. He hoped he'd beat his parents to the ranch, so they wouldn't meet his wife and her sisters before he could properly introduce them.

His gut boiled, because he hadn't told his parents he was actually married to Sarena. The words just hadn't come, and he didn't know how to give that kind of news over the phone anyway.

Sarena had not been terribly happy with him when he'd finally confessed to her that his parents still didn't know they were married. He'd told her while they went through the last of the boxes in the shed on Sunday afternoon, and she'd glared at him.

"You know why we're out here, digging through dirty boxes, right?" she'd asked.

"To find out why your dad changed his will?"

"*Secrets*, Darren." She'd shook her head and rolled her eyes. "You should've told them."

"I'm going to tell them," he said. "When they get here on Thursday."

Thursday had arrived, and Darren really needed to get to Fox Hollow before his mom and dad. Thankfully, as he rounded the bend in the road and the farmhouse came into view, there were no other cars there.

He breathed normally for the first time in twenty minutes, parked, and hurried into the house. Warmth greeted him, as did the scent of roasted turkey, butter, and freshly baked bread. "Wow," he said, drinking in the scene before him.

Everything had been cleaned up, and a new tablecloth sat on the table at the back of the house. Browns, tans, oranges, and yellows assaulted his eyes, from the paper turkeys hanging from the lampshades to the cornucopia in the middle of the table.

"You guys have been busy," he said to the three women in the kitchen. He gave them a smile and quickly kissed Sarena.

"It's all Sorrell," she said. "Did I not mention that she loves holidays? Goes all out?"

"This is not all out," Sorrell said over her shoulder. She whisked something on the stove, and Darren smiled secretly with Seren and Sarena.

"I can't wait to see all out," he said. "Because this is amazing."

"It's a few decorations," Sorrell said.

"And pie," Darren said, spotting the three sitting on the

end of the counter. He went toward them, and Sorrell stepped right in front of him, a very stern look on her face.

"Don't you dare, Mister."

"I just wanna see what kind they are," he said, grinning at her.

"Pumpkin, pecan, and apple," she said. "Now shoo. Go shower or something."

Darren laughed, glad when Sorrell's face cracked into a smile too. "All right. I think I have time." He shot a glance toward the door as he went down the hall, telling himself there was no way his parents would arrive in the next ten minutes. They weren't supposed to be there for another hour, and he could shower.

He still soaped and shaved as fast as he could, rejoining the Adams women in only eight minutes.

"They're not here," Sarena assured him when he came out of the hallway, his eyes already on the door. "If you'd told them about us before this moment, you wouldn't be hopping around like a scared rabbit."

Darren didn't answer, because he didn't want to argue with her in front of her sisters. He didn't need the lecture, he knew that. As he had no role in getting the feast on the table, he headed out the front door and sat on the bench Sarena often did.

Twenty minutes later, his dad's luxury SUV came rolling down the road, and Darren jumped to his feet to go greet them. He was laughing by the time his mother eased out of the passenger seat. "Momma," he said, engulfing her in a tight hug. He closed his eyes and breathed in her maternal scent, happier than he'd anticipated being at seeing her.

"Oh, wow," she said, laughing with him as she patted him on the back. "What a nice welcome." She released him, and he went to embrace his father too.

"You guys made it," he said.

"Yeah, this place is a bit off the beaten path, isn't it?" His dad looked up at the farmhouse.

"So dear," his mother said, linking her arm through his. "This is your girlfriend?" She beamed up at him while Darren tried to get his pulse out of his throat so he could speak. "We're thrilled you're dating again. How has it been going?"

"Great," he said, clearing his throat in the next moment. "And, uh, Momma? Daddy? She's not my girlfriend."

His mother's step faltered. "Then why are we eating here?" she asked. She stopped completely, as if she couldn't go into the farmhouse now.

Darren slipped his arm out of his mother's and faced his parents. He slicked his palms down the front of his jeans. "She's not my girlfriend, because we got married a couple of months ago. Well, like six weeks ago."

"Married?" His father's eyebrows shot straight up under his cowboy hat.

"She's my wife," Darren said with a small smile that was ready to grow, if only his mom didn't look like he'd hit her with a bag of bricks.

"He's certainly moved on, Virginia," Dad said.

"I'm—" Darren didn't want to deny it. He *had* moved on,

and only a smidge of guilt touched his heart because of it. "Different," he finished.

"I'll say," his mother said.

"It's a good different," Darren said. "Come on. Come meet her and her sisters." He started up the steps to the porch, glad when he heard footsteps behind him. He opened the door, his heart back to beating against his tongue.

"They're here," he said, leading everyone down the hall. Sarena came out of the kitchen first. Sorrell wiped her hands, and Seren finished covering a tray of rolls with a towel before she joined them. Darren extended his hand toward Sarena, feeling stronger than ever when her skin met his.

"Momma, Daddy," he said, turning to face them as they came into the farmhouse. "This is Sarena Adams, my wife." He nodded to her, and then them. "My parents, Virginia and Kenneth Dumond."

"So nice to meet you," Sarena said. "Darren speaks highly of you." She stepped into his mother and kissed her cheek, which rendered his mother stiff and still. Sarena shook his father's hand, and Darren watched as the ice melted right off the older man's face.

He tried to hide a smile behind more introductions. "Her sisters," he said. "Sorrell and Serendipity. They live here too."

"Oh, so all of you share the house?" his mother asked as Sorrell and Serendipity shook hands all around.

"That's right," Sarena said. "I own the ranch, and Darren was just living in a cabin. So he moved in with us."

His parents looked like they'd been dunked in cold water.

"Come in," he said. "Come sit down. There's coffee and

sweet tea." As they moved through the living room to the big kitchen and dining room at the back of the house, the back door opened and Theo and Phillip walked in.

Sarena introduced them to Darren's parents, and Sorrell said, "We'll be ready in ten minutes. No pie!" She swatted at Phillip as he got a little too close to her precious pies.

"I told you to put them on the deck," Seren said.

"So the critters can eat them?" Sorrell scoffed, and Sarena shook her head.

Theo stepped over to Sorrell, resting his hand on the small of her back and said, "I can put them in the garage for you, Sorrell."

"Yes, please, Theo," she said, flashing him a smile. Darren met Sarena's eye, and they quickly looked away from each other.

"Yes, please, Theo," he whispered to her as he took a glass of sweet tea to his father, who'd found a spot at the table. "Momma? Coffee?"

"Yes, please, dear," she said.

Darren returned to the kitchen to cater to her needs, thinking the announcement of his marriage had actually gone really well. He'd just set her cup of coffee on the table in front of her when a cry rose into the air.

A shriek, really.

Darren spun back to the kitchen, his heart pounding. The room went completely dark, and he threw his hand out to find the table to support him. He knocked his knuckles against it, which sent a sharp pain up his arm.

"It's okay," someone said. "It was just an accident."

An accident.

Darren got thrown back in time five years as something burnt and acrid filled his nose. He couldn't see. He couldn't hear anything anymore either. The whole world was spinning so fast. Too fast.

The sound of crying met his ears, and someone yelled for someone else to get a towel. Or was it a cloth?

"She's bleeding," he heard, and he wondered if Diana had cried out for help. Had anyone helped her?

He blinked and breathed, trying to get back into the present. His memories and what was happening around him crashed and collided, and Darren couldn't make sense of any of it.

He had to get out of there. Get to Diana.

His vision cleared as he started to move. People clamored around him, some calling out, someone crying, and Darren might've heard his name. But he kept moving. Outside, he fumbled in his pocket for his keys before realizing he didn't have them.

He slowed, the panic that had fired through him only a moment ago ebbing slightly. This was all wrong. Confused, he turned back to the house.

This wasn't his house.

"Come on," Sarena said, coming through the front door he'd left open. "It's going to be okay, Sorrell. Keep the ice on it, Seren." She glanced at Darren as she went past him, but she didn't say anything.

Darren watched the group move down the steps, Theo

never more than a few inches from Sorrell. She wept, a high-pitched whine coming from her mouth every few steps.

He had no idea what had happened. He stood at the top of the steps, trying to find his bearings.

"Will you check the stove and oven?" Sarena called after Sorrell had been loaded into her sedan. Theo got behind the wheel, and Sarena didn't wait for Darren to answer her before she got in the passenger seat.

His parents joined him, and his mother said, "I hope she'll be okay."

"What happened?" Darren asked. He hated that he'd essentially blacked out. He'd been transported to a different time, a different place. Memories zipped around his mind now, because he'd let them out.

"Sorrell picked up the pan of gravy, and it slipped out of her hand," Daddy said. "She got burned, and it looked pretty bad."

"They're taking her to the hospital." Momma put her hand on Darren's arm. "Are you okay, baby? You said something in there I didn't catch, and you're as white as a sheet."

The weight of her gaze on the side of his face made Darren keep staring straight head, watching the sedan round the bend and disappear from sight.

"Come on," Momma said. "Let's go clean up so we can eat when they get back." She turned and headed back inside. Darren finally did too, and he found his mother had stepped right into the kitchen and assumed her role there easily.

She cleaned up the spilled gravy, and Darren watched as she worked off the burnt goop that had landed on the burner.

That was where the smell had come from, and foolishness streamed through him.

Maybe he wasn't as past Diana as he'd thought. Misery laced through him, and he finally got to his feet. "I'm going to go to the hospital," he said. "Will you two be okay here?"

"Yes," Daddy said. "Go on and make sure they're okay."

Darren hurried down the hall to get his keys, and when he returned to the kitchen, Phillip was there, laughing with his dad. They really would be fine.

He strode out the front door, and his skin itched the whole drive into town. He parked near the emergency entrance, thinking he'd jog inside. But his steps slowed the closer to the door he got. He wasn't moving backward, and he did go through it and inside.

Theo sat with Serendipity, the two of them wearing very different expressions. Darren went toward them and sat beside Theo. "What's the news?"

"Haven't heard," he said, and he looked absolutely miserable. Darren had been in the man's boots before, and it hadn't been pleasant.

"Is Sarena back there with her?"

"Yes," Serendipity said. She'd been crying, and Darren understood her anguish too.

He wished he could comfort either one of them, but he simply didn't know how. His emotions ping-ponged all around, and he could barely keep himself in the chair.

After only a few minutes, he couldn't sit there for another moment. "I'm going to go see what I can find out." He walked toward the counter where people checked in. "I just need to talk to Sarena Adams," he said. "She's back there with her sister, and I'll just be a minute." He started for the door to the right of the counter, though the woman said he couldn't.

"Sir," she said as he opened the door and walked past her. "You really can't."

"She's my wife," Darren said, barely slowing. "And she's not the one who's hurt." He glanced over his shoulder at the woman. "It'll be fine."

She let him go, which actually surprised Darren. He walked down the hall bordering a ton of desks and stations, where various nurses and doctors worked. He found Sarena and Sorrell waiting in the third room on the left, and he stepped inside the small room.

"Darren." Sarena catapulted herself out of the chair and into his arms. She clung to him, and Darren sure did like that.

"How are you, Sorrell?" he asked, because he needed to keep a clear head here.

"The doctor just left to get a salve he wants her to use," Sarena said, stepping over to her sister, who had a white cloth over her arm. "He cleaned it, and it's not a super serious burn. He said somewhere between a first degree and a second. He wants to put this salve on it and wrap it, and then we'll be done."

"I'm glad," Darren said. Sorrell's face was too red, and he actually hoped she'd let Theo take care of her for a few days. "Can I talk to you for a second?" He glanced at Sarena and stepped out into the hall, his chest tight.

"What's going on?" she asked, looking up at him with concern.

"I freaked out back there," he said. "I heard *accident*, and all I could think about was Diana." He exhaled and pulled his cowboy hat off his head. Heat filled his face, and a sweat broke out along the back of his neck. "I'm not ready for this."

A keen sense of panic welled in his stomach, pressing up and down and out all at the same time.

"Ready for what?" Sarena asked.

"You deserve someone so much better than me," he said next.

"What are you talking about?"

"I have to go." He started to step past her, but she reached out and put her hand on his arm.

"Darren, wait."

He paused, the urge to get out of this hospital and out of this town overwhelming him. He couldn't stay here. He couldn't watch Sarena get hurt, though some part of him knew he was the one who was about to hurt her.

"Go where?" she asked him.

"I don't know," he said. "I just...I'm not ready for this, and..." He looked at her, his guilt multiplying. "I'm so sorry."

With that, he turned and headed for the exit. Behind him, Sarena called out, "Ready for what?"

Any of it, he thought as he left the hospital. He wasn't ready for any of it.

* * *

An hour later, he pulled into an all-you-can-eat buffet, his parents following him into the lot. He'd managed to get them out of the farmhouse while he grabbed the few essentials he needed to survive for a few days. He could buy clothes, boots, and a new toothbrush.

Truth be told, he could buy a new phone charger too, but he'd grabbed his from the bedroom and stuffed it in his pocket so Phillip and his parents wouldn't know he'd walked out on his wife.

She's not really your wife, he told himself as he parked. Diana was his wife. Diana had been his whole life.

"You can do this," he told himself. "It's one meal. They weren't going to stay overnight anyway." He unbuckled his seat belt and made a show of looking for something in his truck, though his wallet sat in his back pocket. "Just go eat with them, and then figure out what to do."

Sarena was right. He didn't know where to go. He had nowhere to go. He just knew he couldn't go back to the farmhouse and eat Thanksgiving dinner with a weepy, burnt Sorrell. He couldn't pretend he hadn't run from the house at the first sign of trauma. He couldn't keep thinking he'd become someone else, when he was still the same broken, beaten, and bruised man he'd been since the day Diana had died.

CHAPTER 22

"But what did he say?" Sarena stood on the back deck with Phillip while Serendipity worked in the kitchen to get the hot foods hot again. Theo and Sorrell sat on the couch together, and while Sarena hated seeing her sister in pain, at least it had brought her and Theo closer.

"He said you guys were going to be a while," Phillip said. "And he said they should just go to a restaurant for Thanksgiving dinner. Then they left."

"Did he take anything with him?" Sarena couldn't believe Darren had left. Just left. He'd walked out at the hospital, but she'd fully expected to find him at the farmhouse when she returned.

"Not that I could tell." Phillip shrugged, clearly not getting the gravity of the situation.

Sarena nodded, because there wasn't much else she could do. Phillip stepped around her and went back inside, but

Sarena lingered on the deck, staring up into the leafless trees. "What do I do now?"

Darren would surely be back soon. She'd barely gotten to meet his parents, and even when he'd been angry with her, he'd come home.

But as she stood there, she had the very real feeling that he wouldn't be coming home that night. Sighing and determined to deal with this once dinner had ended, she went back inside.

"Five minutes," Seren said. "I'm just waiting on the rolls now."

"Okay." Sarena didn't slow as she went through the kitchen and down the hall. In their bedroom, nothing seemed out of the ordinary. Drawers weren't thrown open, and in fact, all of Darren's clothes and boots and hats were still there.

"Surely he'll come home." She checked the bathroom, and everything of his remained. She glanced at the outlet, noticing that his phone charger wasn't there. Sarena's stomach lurched and dropped, and her ribs seemed to collapse in on her organs, crushing them.

"Ready," Seren called. "Sarena? We're ready to eat."

She couldn't keep her family waiting, but she did take a moment to think about what Darren had said about family. *A family is something you choose, not something you're born into.*

She chose Sorrell and Serendipity, Theo and Phillip. She wanted to choose Darren, but he'd obviously chosen something else.

Sadness accompanied her down the hall to the kitchen, where everyone stood around the island, waiting for her. "Sorry," she said, her voice almost cracking in her chest.

"I'm sorry I ruined Thanksgiving," Sorrell said.

"You didn't," Seren and Sarena said together. "Now come on," Seren added. "Who's going to say grace so we can eat while the food is hot?"

"Where did Darren go?" Sorrell asked.

Sarena closed her eyes and said, "I'll say grace." Anything would be better than talking about Darren.

THE NEXT MORNING, Sarena woke alone, and while she'd done it for years and years of her life, she now knew how wonderful it was to wake up with her husband beside her. The fact that Darren wasn't there hurt so much she couldn't get a decent breath.

She'd called and texted him last night, after the food had been eaten and the leftovers put away. He hadn't answered, and she'd actually slept on his side of the bed just so she could have the scent of him in every breath.

Pathetic, she knew.

But she didn't care if she was pathetic if it brought Darren home. As she showered, got her prosthetic in place, dressed, and went down the hall to the kitchen, she wondered if he thought of the farmhouse as his home. He didn't have a problem leaving his stuff around the house, and he'd never once complained about her sisters living with them.

She pulled out her phone and sent him a text. *Can you please let me know that you're okay?*

Another one. *And when you're coming home. And where*

you went. And why. Is it because Sorrell and Seren live here with us?

She erased all of that before she sent the text, her indecision raging through her.

In the end, she said, *I miss you. I'm going to talk to Uncle Dale today. Can't wait to tell you about it.*

Her sisters would sleep late today, as neither of them had to work, and Sarena managed to brew coffee, sip a cup, and feed Darren's dog before getting up to leave the house. She didn't see Sorrell or Seren, and poor Koda looked so dejected as he followed Sarena toward the front door.

"You wanna come?" she asked him. His tail wagged, and though Sarena knew that was universal dog language, she took it as a yes. "Come on, then," she said. "You can ride in the back seat."

The dog bolted from the house when Sarena opened the door, and she got him loaded in the back seat. But he didn't stay there. He promptly climbed over the middle console and sat in the passenger seat while she buckled herself behind the wheel. "You're trouble," she told him. "But you can chase Uncle Dale's chickens." She grinned at the golden retriever, the wicked thought of letting Koda catch one of her uncle's prized chickens really appealing.

She wouldn't, of course. She drove down the lane and turned onto the highway. Her uncle had never been married—at least Sarena thought he hadn't. When she'd found the marriage certificate, that had changed. But he'd never been married since her mother that she knew of. Her mind played with that thought, and she wondered if he'd loved her mother so much that he couldn't get married again.

"Maybe he's like Darren," she murmured, the sentence making her so sad. She hadn't realized Darren's odd behavior yesterday during Sorrell's spill, but Phillip had told her about it.

He just sort of froze, Phillip had said. He might've yelled something. There was a lot going on.

Sarena had found him on the front porch, and he'd definitely been a strange shade of gray. She'd just thought he couldn't stomach the sight of an injury.

"If that were true," she said. "He wouldn't be able to look at your foot." And he had. Lots of times. Sarena suspected his injuries were mental and not physical, and that he'd run because he needed some space to figure things out.

She could give him space, if she knew he was okay. Her phone chimed from its spot in the cup holder, and she picked it up though she had a strict rule for not looking at her device while driving.

I'm okay.

Relief rushed through her. Darren was okay. He didn't say anything else, and Sarena pressed her lips together and put her phone down.

Her uncle lived on the north side of town, in a neighborhood made up of several blocks of homes that had been built seventy or eighty years ago. They were all made of brick, either white, yellow, or red. Every now and then, someone had gone wild and painted their bricks blue, but for the most part, this part of town should probably be razed and rebuilt.

The lawns stretched toward the street, with the homes farther back off the road. They all had a tiny cement pad for a porch, and they were all square. Most of the driveways were made of dirt, and that was what she pulled onto as she turned toward her uncle's house.

His bricks had been white at some point in the past. Now, they seemed to have a yellow-brown tint to them, especially where the water dripped off the roof and splashed the ground below.

Sarena parked her car and looked at the lawn. With December nearly upon them, the grass had stopped growing. Not that Uncle Dale mowed it in the spring, summer, or autumn. But someone had been by to trim the grass enough to get by. It was far longer than Sarena would've left it, but this wasn't her house.

"Okay," she said, sighing. "We're here." But she still didn't get out. Uncle Dale had left a lawn chair near the porch, but weeds had grown all around it, which meant he hadn't sat there in some time.

Two trees grew in the front yard, but not because Uncle Dale took care of them. He didn't take care of anything.

"Let's go," she said to Koda. She got out of the car, surprised when the dog followed her across the driver's seat. She supposed Darren didn't take him in a car very often, and the little pup didn't know he should go to the back to get out. "I'll train you up," she said to him. "Now stay by me."

She hadn't brought a leash or anything, but Koda went with her down the sidewalk and up the steps. She knocked, because Uncle Dale didn't have a doorbell.

"Comin'," he yelled from somewhere inside the house, and she didn't think it was big enough to warrant standing on the steps for a full minute before the door opened. "Oh." Uncle Dale held onto the door for support, his eyes locked onto Sarena's. "What can I do for you?"

"I'm not a traveling salesman," Sarena said, her wit and irritation with him combining into something she needed to learn to tame. She pulled in a breath. "I mean, I wanted to talk to you about a few things."

"What kind of things?"

"My mother," Sarena said. "Your marriage to my mother. My father's will. Those kind of things." She watched as Uncle Dale's mouth fell open. He stumbled back a step, and Sarena lurched forward as if she could catch and then hold his bulk.

Thankfully, he didn't need her to, but it allowed enough space for her to get through the door and into the house. "Come on, Koda."

The dog entered slowly, almost testing his weight on each paw as he entered the house. Sarena could smell something foul, and for Koda, that was probably a signal that he should tread carefully.

The house was basically a square cut into fourths. One fourth for the living room, right up front. One fourth for the kitchen and dining area, in the back. A hallway led back to one bathroom and a bedroom in the back fourth. And another bedroom in the front fourth.

Uncle Dale had not cleaned any of it in a very long time. Sarena acted like she couldn't see the mess or smell whatever had rotted, and she rounded the couch and perched delicately on the edge of it. Koda stayed right by her, looking up at her as if to ask, *Why did you make me come here? This isn't fun.*

No, it was not fun. She reached down and stroked his head as Uncle Dale shuffled and limped his way to his nest. The recliner squeaked as he collapsed into it, and Sarena was surprised it still rocked.

"So you know I was married to your mother," he said.

"Yes," she said. "I found the marriage certificate."

Uncle Dale wore fire in his expression, and Sarena hadn't seen him like that before. "She was mine first, you know. Then Will had to come back from Korea and steal her away from me."

"Is that why you two don't talk?"

"One of the reasons. The biggest reason."

"He's my father, though," Sarena said.

"We didn't know that," Uncle Dale said. "For a long, long time. We didn't know. Sue always said you were his, but neither of us really knew. We didn't know how she could know. She called it a gut feeling." He scoffed, as if guts were never right.

Sarena just watched him. He practically pulsed with an energy she could only classify as angry. "Is that why you had Daddy change the will?"

"That ranch was mine first," Uncle Dale said. "I lived there for twenty months with your mother. We were going to build our life there."

Sarena let the tension bleed through her, expecting to fire something back at him. All she felt was compassion for the life

Uncle Dale had wanted, but lost. "I'm sorry, Uncle Dale," she said.

He clearly hadn't anticipated her saying that either, because he opened his mouth but closed it again quickly.

"So Daddy changed the will, because neither of you were sure who was my father," she said. "And put in the clause that said one of us girls had to get married to keep the ranch."

"Yes," he said. "Because Sue only specified the oldest daughter, and Will and I fought over who that was."

"But it would've been me no matter what," Sarena said, frowning. "Right? I mean, if I'm yours, I'm still the oldest daughter."

"Only with the outdated will," he said. "But Susan had notarized another one, naming your father as the inheritor of the ranch, and directing him to pass it to 'their' oldest daughter. That could've been Sorrell."

"When did you get the paternity test done?"

"I didn't," Uncle Dale said. "Will did that."

"Why didn't he change the will afterward?" All of this could've been avoided had her father just updated his will. He obviously knew how.

"Oh, the law firm we'd used closed when the partners moved, and he was so busy with the ranch, and then he got sick. I guess he just forgot."

"You didn't forget, though, did you?"

"Of course I didn't forget." He glared at her. "Doesn't matter now anyway. You went and got yourself married."

Sarena's heart shriveled, but she just nodded. She looked steadily back at her uncle, only compassion and empathy for him. She thought that was strange, but she couldn't change it. She cocked her head. "Did you fight for my mother?"

"Fight for her?"

"Yeah, you know, go to her and tell her you loved her, and it was supposed to be your life on the ranch, and to not run off with Daddy?"

Uncle Dale folded in on himself in less time than it took to breathe out. Sarena didn't need to hear a vocal answer, because she'd seen the "no" in her uncle's demeanor.

"Did you ever wonder if it would've been different if you had?" she asked.

"Every day," he mumbled.

Her heart cracked for him—and for herself. She couldn't just let Darren walk away from her. She couldn't allow him to send two-word texts and be done.

She didn't want to be done.

"What would you do with the ranch now, Uncle Dale? You're not fit to work it."

"I know." He nodded, all of his bravado and anger gone. "Honestly, I'd probably honor Sue's wishes."

"And give it to me."

"Yes," he said. "And give it to you."

A calm understanding passed between them, and Sarena stood up. "I really am sorry, Uncle Dale. My mother...I didn't get to know her as well as I would've liked, but I didn't know she could do something like this to a person."

"She followed her heart," he said, struggling to get out of the recliner.

"Stay," she said. "I'll let myself out." She snapped at Koda, who'd already stood up to go with her. She walked around the couch and opened the front door. Koda streaked outside, his tail low, but Sarena paused and looked back at her uncle.

"You should come out to Fox Hollow for Christmas," she said. "Tell us some stories of our mother and what your life was like on the ranch during those twenty months."

His whole face lit up. "You think so?"

"I'll invite Aunt Scottie too," she said. "You get along with her, don't you?"

"She's all right," Uncle Dale said. "It's probably time to forgive and forget. I'm gettin' too old to hold so tightly to ancient grudges."

Sarena smiled and nodded. "All right. I'll tell Sorrell, and she'll make sure we have enough candied ham." With that, she left, pulling the door closed behind her. "Koda," she called as she went down the steps, and the little puppy ran toward her from the house across the street.

She loaded him into the car, turned the key in the ignition, and called Darren.

She was *not* going to be grumpy Aunt Sarena, old and hobbling around on her one good foot while she lamented the time she'd let the one she loved get away from her without a fight.

No, she was not.

Darren didn't answer his phone.

CHAPTER 23

Brian stared at his phone, sure he'd seen the wrong words. His eyes had just rearranged all the letters to read *Take me to dinner tonight?* with Serendipity's name on the text.

His heart thumped like nothing he'd ever experienced before, and he hurried to call her.

"Hey," she said easily, as if she hadn't just agreed to go out with him—*really* out with him—in a text.

"Are you serious?" he asked.

"About what?"

"Going to dinner tonight." He glanced around, though no one should be nearby. The sun had started to go down, and he'd been the only one left out with the cattle hours ago.

"Yes," she said. "I need a break from the farmhouse, and I've already told my sisters I'm going to a movie by myself."

A smile lit up Brian's whole soul. *Thank you, Lord*, he thought. His next thoughts became how he could get back to his cabin faster, but he was at least thirty minutes away. "Well, we can eat and go to a movie if you want," he said, heading for the ATV he'd left parked at the edge of the field. "I'm at least an hour from being ready though."

"I'll look something up for us," she said. "And I'll meet you at the highway."

"All right." Brian's fantasies about what that night would be dried up slightly. He wouldn't get to pull down the dirt lane, and ring the doorbell to collect Serendipity from her house.

Okay, fine. He wouldn't die. And maybe one day in the future, he could. *One day soon*, he thought. *Okay, Lord? One day soon.*

"Great, see you in an hour." The line went dead, and Brian didn't even mind Serendipity's abrupt way of ending phone calls. He jogged toward the ATV now, and kept the throttle open as far as it would go the whole way back to the ranch. He filled out the paperwork quickly, knowing he'd have to redo it tomorrow.

He just had to get out of there.

At the cabin, Tomas had already showered and had his feet on the coffee table in front of him, the TV blaring something.

"I'm showering and heading out after," Brian said, continuing from the back door to the hallway. Tomas yelled something to him, but Brian slammed the bathroom door and showered in record time.

"Gonna be late," he said, grabbing his keys by the front door and rushing out despite Tomas's question of, "Late for what?"

The door closed between them, and a slight stab of guilt hit Brian in the gut. Not enough to make him go back and tell Tomas anything though.

"Maybe you can kiss her tonight," he told himself as he made the drive over to Fox Hollow. He had to go back to the junction about five or ten minutes, and then come back up another road another five or ten minutes.

Seren waited on a fallen log in the bare spot of land between tons of trees. She looked up when he pulled in, and she gave him no time to get out of the truck and greet her, hug her, kiss her, or help her into the truck.

"Hey," she said, sliding onto the seat almost the moment he put the truck in park. "Ready?

"Yes," he said, telling himself to calm down. It was obvious he liked this woman much more than she liked him. He hated being on the wrong side of that equation, and he forced himself to lower the wattage on his smile. "What movie are we seeing?"

"How do you feel about rewatching a classic?" she asked.

He didn't care what they watched. She'd be at his side, and he could hold her hand. Or put his arm around her shoulders. Again, he coached himself to slow down. *Slow way down, cowboy.*

"Which one?" he asked.

"Annie?"

"Oh, I saw they were showing that at the Main Street theater for a few weeks. That's fine."

"Our tickets are at eight-forty."

"So plenty of time for dinner."

"Yeah," she said. "And I'm feeling very much like pasta tonight."

"Poco Loco?" he asked.

"Wondering what you think about trying Elbows and Orzo."

"What and what?"

"It's a new place," she said. "Not in Chestnut Springs. It's all pasta dishes, from elbow macaroni to sausage orzo soup."

"Sounds amazing," he said. "You know where it is? We have time to get there and back?"

"Yeah," she said. "It's just over in Clydesdale."

"Oh, ten minutes."

"You got it." Serendipity smiled at him and ran her fingers through her dark hair. Brian really wanted to do that too, but he kept both hands on the wheel.

"Why did you need to get out of the farmhouse tonight?" he asked.

She cut a look at him. "If I tell you, you can't tell anyone."

"Who am I going to tell?"

"Uh, Tomas," she said, giggling. "Or Aaron. Or Seth, or Russ, or Travis, or—"

"Okay," he said, laughing too. "I won't tell anyone."

"Or Darren," she said. "Because it's about Darren."

"What about Darren?"

"Do you know where he is?"

Brian looked at her, confused. "He lives with you."

"He left yesterday when Sorrell got burned. He hasn't come back, and Sarena is beside herself." She sighed like her sister had no right to be upset when her husband had left her. In that moment, Brian wondered if Serendipity was even capable of an emotional relationship with him. He'd already dived in and was treading water, and it felt like she was still sitting on the pool deck, trying to decide if he was worth getting wet for.

"I haven't heard from him," Brian said.

"Neither have we. Well, he did text Sarena this morning to say he was okay. We've been planning a way for her to get him back all day." She groaned. "*Allllll day*, Brian."

He smiled, despite the needling worry in his lungs. "So you need a break."

"And carbs," she said. "And buttery popcorn."

"You shall have it all, my dear." They laughed together, and Brian decided not to make any firm decisions about her or their relationship just yet.

They arrived at Elbows & Orzo, where Brian found a grilled cheese sandwich that had pulled pork, tons of cheddar cheese, *and* macaroni and cheese between two slices of bread. His idea of heaven.

So was the conversation. The gorgeous woman across from him. He held her hand on the way out of the restaurant, and she seemed to like it. At least she didn't mind.

They drove back to Chestnut Springs, the easy vibe between them continuing. He bought popcorn, candy, and sodas, and they took their seats in the semi-dark theater.

This was definitely a date. He could definitely kiss her tonight. They could officially be *some*thing. He didn't mind the texting and secret meetings they'd been doing for the last five or six weeks, but he could admit he was ready to graduate to something else.

She reached for his hand once they'd finished their dessert of popcorn and licorice, and Brian wasn't even sure who Annie was in that moment.

Afterward, he drove her back to the ranch, and he pulled into the hiding spot they usually used. "You don't have to walk back," he said. "I can take you."

She swung her face toward him, and Brian thought he saw attraction in her eyes. It was dark and hard to tell, though. "I can walk," she said, reaching for the door handle.

He jumped out of the truck too, rounding it to cut her off before she disappeared again. "Serendipity," he said, almost yelling her name. He caught her hand, and time stilled for a moment. "When can I see you again?" he asked. "When can we do *this* again?"

"I don't know," she said.

Brian couldn't let the opportunity go. He gathered her into his arms slowly, willing to let her slip away from him if she wanted to. She didn't. A sigh moved through his body. He wanted to tell her he liked her, but he thought it was pretty obvious.

She wrapped her arms around him too, and Brian's skin crackled with energy. He pulled back slightly, ready to kiss her and claim her as his. Desperate for it.

But Serendipity's eyes widened. She stiffened. She pulled away. "I should go."

"Serendipity," he said, foolishness clawing through him

with the strength of a backhoe. "What's—I mean. What have I done wrong?"

"Nothing," she said. "I'm just not ready to kiss you." She offered him a small smile he could barely see before she turned away from him and walked right on down the road.

Brian stayed near the tree trunks until he couldn't hear her footsteps anymore. He wished the idiocy running through his veins would disappear as easily as Serendipity seemed to be able to. It lingered with him all the way back to Chestnut Ranch, even accompanying him down the hall to his bedroom, going so far as to crawl into bed with him.

"What do I need to do?" he asked the ceiling, really hoping the words would go all the way to the Lord's ears. "For her to be ready to kiss me?"

CHAPTER 24

S erendipity spent the weekend at Fox Hollow, her phone silent. She could get lost inside her own mind very easily sometimes, especially when she had something big to think about.

And Brian Gray was a very big thing. Rather, *dating* Brian Gray was a very big thing.

When she'd spoken to her sisters again on Saturday morning, she learned that Sarena had a plan to drive to Frio on Monday and get Darren back.

"I at least have to fight for him," she said. "For us."

Sorrell had agreed, and Serendipity just wanted Sarena to be happy. So she'd gone along with the crazy idea too. Never mind that Sarena couldn't drive for long distances very well, and the fact that she didn't even know where Darren's parents lived.

"It's a small town," Sorrell had said. "You'll stop someone you see and ask them."

Serendipity had almost started laughing. Sarena didn't approach strangers very easily. She did manage the ranch extremely well, and that included the two cowboys she'd given the weekend off.

Seren suspected that Sarena was hoping Darren would return to Fox Hollow before Monday, and she wouldn't have to make the journey.

But he didn't.

She met her sister in the kitchen, glad someone had already made coffee. "Ready to go?" she asked Sarena, who actually startled at the sound of Serendipity's voice.

"What? Oh, yes. I'm ready."

"Go slow," Serendipity said, sitting down at the table with her. "You'll be fine."

"You love him," Sorrell said. "Remember to lead with that." She nodded like Sarena had this in the bag, but one look at her sister's green face, and Serendipity thought it would be a miracle if she even made it to Frio.

"I wish I could go with you," she said, though she didn't wish any such thing. "I've got four tours today."

"So you'll be late," Sorrell said.

"Yes," Seren confirmed. "And I think I'm going to stop by Elbows and Orzo on the way home. So don't count on me for dinner."

"I've wanted to try that place," Sorrell said.

"Me too," Serensaid, hating the lie as it came out. But it wasn't really a lie. She *had* wanted to try the pasta place. And she had. They didn't need to know she'd already eaten there. "I'll bring you something."

"Would you?" Sorrell grinned at Seren with such appreciation in her eyes. "That would be great. Thanks, Seren."

"Sure," she said. "Well, I better go." Only so she wouldn't keep lying to her sisters.

Seren called Brian once her phone had connected to her car. "Hey," she said when he answered. "Fancy taking me to that pizza place in Austin?"

"Tonight?" he asked.

"Yeah," she said. "I only have three tours today, and I'm done by thirty-forty-five."

"Let me see what I can do," he said. "I'll call you back."

Seren reached out and tapped the screen to end the call, her guts writhing. She *had* lied to her sisters when she'd said she had the late tour. And she was keeping Brian on a string. She knew that. He dropped everything when she called, and while she'd liked that at first, now it made her feel like she was taking advantage of him.

They'd only texted a few times over the weekend, and that was unusual too.

She'd spoken true on Friday night when she said she wasn't ready to kiss him yet, and she hadn't had the courage to stay and see his face for how he felt about that. He was obviously ready to kiss her.

Maybe she should break up with him. But was there anything to break up over? They'd been to one dinner and one movie.

Around and around her mind went, just as it had been for forty-eight hours now. She completed her tours, the script and answers so easy because she'd said them thousands of times.

She changed out of her brown Texas Parks shirt and into a cute, flowery blouse before heading out to her car.

Brian could pick her up at the visitor's center, something they'd arranged earlier in the day when he'd texted to say he could be done at four.

She drove down to the visitor's center parking lot and sat in the car, catching up with her email and social media on her phone until Brian arrived.

She warred with herself, a loud voice in her ear telling her to end things with him that night. If she didn't, she knew she'd start to fall for him. In a lot of ways, she already had. She just wasn't as emotional as her sisters—as a lot of women.

Brian didn't seem to care, and Seren wondered if he really could like her enough to stay with her for longer than a few weeks. No other man had.

Why is he any different? she wondered, immediately banishing the fatalistic thought.

He could be, she told herself instead. He really could be.

Someone knocked on her window, startling her. She looked over to find Brian's handsome face smiling at her. Her heart knocked around a couple of times in her chest as she drank in his dark eyes and that sexy beard. He wore his cowboy hat, of course, and tonight, he wore a red and black striped shirt, with squares of cream in between all the boxes the stripes made.

"Hey," she said, easing out of her car. "Sorry, I got absorbed on my phone."

"It's fine." He didn't move to hold her hand or give her a

hello hug. Her lungs iced over, and she had to break through the constraints to be able to breathe. "Your car is okay here?"

"Yeah," she said. "It'll be fine." She followed him to his truck just a couple of parking spots over, trying to imagine what kissing him would be like.

Seren had only kissed two other men, and one of them had laughed at her immediately afterward. Would Brian laugh too?

She wanted to slam on the brakes of this relationship, and it hadn't even started yet. But if she slammed hard enough now, she wouldn't get hurt later.

She'd just tell him tonight, after the pizza. The words started forming in her head, and they took all the way to Austin to come together.

Look, Brian, I don't think this is going to work out...

"Ready, sweetheart?" he asked her, and the sentence shattered. She looked at him, and she couldn't find an ounce of malice or ingenuity anywhere in him. Maybe she could just see where this dinner took them. Maybe they could have a real relationship...

Seren would have to wait and see—and pray that she wouldn't lose her heart to the handsome cowboy.

CHAPTER 25

Darren had spent the past three days either on horseback, lounging in a chair as he studied the Texas wilderness, or sleeping in a tent.

He hadn't been able to answer his parents' questions about why he'd come home with them instead of staying at Fox Hollow, and after he'd texted Sarena to say he was okay, he couldn't stand to have service and not be talking to her.

He'd packed a tent and a chair, along with the clothes he'd bought on Friday, into his old Boy Scout backpack and saddled a horse from his father's stable. He was probably only a few hours away from civilization, but it felt like he was the last man on Earth.

Snickers, his horse, snacked on the winter grass, and Darren stared. The hours passed easily, surprisingly, and he wondered if this could just be his life now. He could go to the grocery store every week or so and head back out to the tent he'd set up in the shade of some trees along the Frio River.

Easy. No complications. No job. No worries. No injuries. No blackouts or split memories or regrets.

"But what kind of life is that?" he asked himself, and not for the first time. He just felt so lost. When Diana had died, he felt like this too. But he'd stayed within the circle of his friends and family. For as long as he could, anyway.

A strong thread of loneliness pulled through him, and Darren needed someone to talk to. He'd left Koda at Fox Hollow, and he thought if he had his dog, he'd be able to live this hermit lifestyle.

The idea of being a hermit reminded him of Sarena's father, who then reminded him of Sarena, of course.

Everything came back to Sarena. It had for months, since he'd first seen her sobbing her eyes out on the day her father had died.

He'd used his knowledge of what it looked like, felt like, and sounded like to lose someone to death's strong grip for good then. Why did it have to haunt him so terribly at other times?

Why hadn't he mastered how to tame those emotions yet? What would it take to properly cage the memories so he could help in a crisis instead of adding trauma to it?

Guilt laced her way through him, and Darren was well-acquainted with her. Guilt that he hadn't been there to help Diana out of the office connected to the paper mill where she worked. Guilt that he got to live when her life had been cut short. Guilt that his ranch had been worth so much, when others worked their whole lives and could still barely afford to buy shoes.

So much guilt.

He closed his eyes and tipped his head back. The sun shone weakly down on the ground, speckling his face through the branches of the winter trees. "Now what?" he asked the Lord. "I can't really stay here." He opened his eyes to the absolute blueness of the sky. "Can I?"

Of course he couldn't. He was married to Sarena Adams, and he did love her. At some point, he'd have to call upon his courage and face her.

"Doesn't have to be today," he muttered to himself, though a frown pulled at his eyebrows that he wasn't already on his way back to Fox Hollow. "Just take the time you need."

The therapist he'd seen exactly once after Diana's death had told him that. Darren wasn't sure if he'd ever taken the time he needed or not. He'd stayed in Frio for a while, only leaving when he couldn't stand to see his wife's bulbs poking their leaves and stems through the ground. They got a fresh start at life every spring, and she didn't.

He'd packed his truck with everything he could take with him, kissed his parents and said goodbye to his siblings, and left. He had a job in Chestnut Springs already, but he hadn't sold the ranch yet. Everything had worked out.

Would it this time too? If so, what did that look like?

Snickers lifted his head, and Darren looked over at the horse as his bridle jangled. He stared at something across the field from where Daren had set up camp, and Darren followed the horse's gaze.

"There's nothing there," he told the equine. The horse

held statue-still, though, his ears the only part of him flicking. He could definitely hear something.

Darren searched the horizon again, but there wasn't anything there. He closed his eyes, and he wasn't sure if that made the sound louder, or if it had simply come closer. But without the aid of his sight, he could definitely hear something.

A buzzing sound that gradually turned into the whine of a motor. Not a car or a truck, but an ATV. Darren had maneuvered one at Chestnut Ranch plenty of times to know.

He opened his eyes again, his muscles tensing as if they'd need to be ready for a fight. He was probably trespassing, and he could pack up his tent and sleeping bag and be gone in ten minutes. Nothing anyone needed to get excited about.

The ATV broke through the trees a few seconds later, but Darren didn't move. Maybe if he stayed still, they wouldn't see him. A ridiculous idea, but Darren had had a lot of those lately.

The person seemed to know exactly where he was, and they came straight for him. When they were about halfway across the field, Darren got up and walked toward Snickers, who put off a nervous energy to have the ATV aiming straight for him. "Whoa," he said to the horse, taking the reins in his fist. "You're okay."

He stood in front of the horse, trying to figure out who drove the ATV. They wore jeans and a black jacket, with a cowboy hat on their head. Could be anyone. He didn't know everyone in Frio anymore, only those who'd lived here longer than the dirt had.

This person wasn't that old, he could tell that much. The ATV slowed, the sound of the engine waning as they came to a stop at least a hundred yards away. Darren widened his stance, ready for anything. Or at least that was what he told himself. In truth, Darren would just pack up and go.

"Hello, there," he called out as the person started walking toward him. He kept his head down, his cowboy had concealing his face. Darren's heart started pounding, because he knew that gait.

Sarena could disguise her body with bulky clothes and hide her face with a too-big hat. But she couldn't change her stride, and the reins fell from Darren's fingers.

He found himself walking toward her too, then breaking into a jog. When they were only ten feet apart, he stopped. She did too, finally lifting her eyes to his. Everything inside him moved frantically. His thoughts couldn't settle, and therefore his brain didn't give his limbs or his voice any directions.

"You're a very hard man to track down, Darren Dumond," she finally said.

He asked the first thing that came into his mind. "What are you doing here?"

"I came to find out if my husband was okay," she said. Even from the shadows of that hat hiding her face, she could get her annoyance across quite well. Her concern too. "I came because I miss you. I came because I need you at Fox Hollow. I came because I love you, and I can't just let you walk out of my life with a terrible explanation and no date for when you'll be back."

With every word she spoke, Darren's heart thawed a little

more. It started to beat better, pumping more blood through his body and up into his brain. Everything simply worked better when he was with Sarena.

"Your mother said you didn't want to be disturbed, and I respect that," she said. "Honestly, I do. But I got on that death trap and drove out here, because you need to know that I'm not going to give up on us. So if you want to live in a tent out here, that's fine. I brought Koda with me, and I'll bring him out to you. You can walk away from me and Fox Hollow, all your friends at Chestnut, and my sisters. That's fine. But you'll have to do it knowing *exactly* how I feel."

He looked at the ATV, his mind finally seizing onto something. "You don't like driving the ATV?"

"I hate it," she said.

I came because I love you.

"I don't want to live in a tent." Darren felt dangerously close to breaking wide open.

"Then come home," Sarena said. She reached her hand toward him, and he wondered if it really would be as easy as taking two steps and putting his hand in hers.

Find out, he thought, and he managed to take the two steps. Reach for her too.

And just like that, he did it.

"I'm sorry," he said.

"Nothing to be sorry about," she said. "I think you need someone to need you, Darren, and I do."

"You're more than capable of running Fox Hollow without me." In fact, he didn't even work there.

"I don't need you for the ranch," she said. "I need you, because I'm not complete without you."

He gazed down at her, this amazing creature who seemed to know exactly what to say. "I left because I love you," he said. "And I didn't want to saddle you with a weak husband who still has panic attacks about the day his wife died. Five years ago."

She reached up and ran her hand along the side of his face. He tried not to lean into the touch, but he failed. Because he needed this woman in his life too, and he craved her touch. "You're not weak," she said. "I think that's called being human." She smiled at him, and Darren wanted to pause time and look at her like this forever.

"Can you forgive me?" he asked.

"Oh, if I have to." She giggled, and Darren swept her into his arms, dislodging her ridiculously huge cowboy hat. She squealed then and wrapped her legs around his waist. Darren's gratitude overwhelmed him, and he said, "Thank you."

Sarena didn't ask him what for. She probably knew he was talking to the Lord. She leaned down, cupping his face in both of her hands, and kissed him. "Come home, cowboy," she whispered before matching her mouth to his again.

Okay, Darren thought. *I will.*

CHAPTER 26

Sarena enjoyed kissing her husband more than anything else in the world. She liked the slow way he moved, like he had nothing better to do than kiss her. She'd gotten him to take the ATV back to his parents' farm, and she'd ridden Snickers. Thankfully. She could still feel the vibrations from the engine in her bones, and she hated it.

When he'd asked her why, she'd told him that she'd lost her foot in an ATV accident. He hadn't known, and he'd apologized at least a dozen times.

But Sarena didn't need his apologies. She needed *him*.

He'd been staying with his parents, and by the time they got back to the farm, she didn't want to make the drive back to Chestnut Springs. She'd hardly been sleeping since he'd left, and she just wanted to sleep.

His mother had begged them to stay at the farm, where Darren had been. But Sarena wanted to make love to her husband, and she didn't want to do that in his childhood bedroom, with his parents down the hall.

She wasn't sure why. They made love with her sisters down the hall.

She broke the kiss, and asked, "Should we get our own place?"

"Mm?" Darren asked, his lips moving to her neck.

"Darren," she said, though she wanted him to keep going. "I think we need our own place."

He lifted his head and looked into her eyes. "At Fox Hollow?"

"Yeah, at Fox Hollow." She ran her fingers through his hair. "There's room on the ranch for another house."

"Oh, easily." He searched her face. "Why do you want one?"

"Privacy," she said. "And as a place to raise our family."

"Family?" he asked, a little too much air in his voice for Sarena's liking.

"I doubt I'll be able to have many kids," she said. "But I'd kind of like at least one. Someone to pass the ranch to."

"I think I could handle one," he said.

"You don't like kids?"

"I like other people's kids," he said.

"How did I not know this about you?"

"Because, sweetheart, we got married to satisfy the conditions of a will." He grinned at her and kissed her again. "I've never thought of myself as father material," he said.

"You'd be a great father," she whispered. "Maybe we could have two kids."

"Oh, you're pushing it now," he teased, claiming her mouth again. "Let's start with one."

"Mm." She tipped her head back so he'd kiss her neck again, which he did. "All right, cowboy. Let's get started." She giggled as he growled, and after he'd made love to her, Sarena lay in the circle of his arms while he slept, wondering how in the world she'd convinced a man like him to marry a woman like her.

She felt like the luckiest woman in the world, and she thanked the Lord for a crazy stipulation in a five-year-old will that should've been fixed but hadn't been.

* * *

THE DAYS and weeks passed back in Chestnut Springs, and life got back to normal at Fox Hollow Ranch. As normal as they'd ever been since mid-October, when Sarena and Darren had gotten married on the back deck.

"Have you noticed anything weird about Seren?" Sarena asked.

Sorrell mixed melted white chocolate over a batch of freshly popped popcorn. She made the delicious, salty-and-sweet treat for her coworkers every year. Sarena would sneak a few bites too, but right now, her attention centered on Serendipity.

"Weird?" Sorrell asked, glancing up quickly.

"She's always doing something at night," Sarena said, looking at the hallway leading to the front door as if her youngest sister would walk in at any moment. But she wouldn't, because she'd said she was doing a painting class at the art supply store. "Or working late. Or going to movies by herself."

Sorrell poured out the chocolate popcorn onto the waiting piece of parchment paper. "You're right. I guess I hadn't thought about it, but she has been gone a lot in the evenings lately."

"For a few weeks now," Sarena said. "Maybe longer."

"Why are you concerned about it?" Sorrell turned to put the dirty bowl in the sink. She faced Sarena again. "Do you think she's hiding something from us?"

"Yes," Sarena said, seizing onto the words. "That's exactly what I think."

Sorrell frowned. "Like what?"

"I have no idea." Sarena sighed and reached for a few kernels of popcorn. "But it's something." She chomped through her popcorn. "What about you and Theo?"

Sorrell just shrugged, and that summed everything up. "How's the house coming?"

"Haven't really started yet," she said. "We just called an architectural firm, and they assigned us to someone." She watched her sister, searching for any signs of distress. "You're okay with me moving out, aren't you?"

"I've said yes a thousand times."

"Sorrell," Sarena said. "I worry about you."

"I know that," Sorrell said. "And I don't need it, Sarena. Honestly, I don't." She turned and pulled a paper towel off the roll, the conversation clearly over.

"Okay," Sarena said. "I'll try to stop."

The back door opened, and Darren walked in wearing a brown leather jacket with his jeans, cowboy boots, and hat, making him the most delicious cowboy in five counties. "Hey," she said, smiling as he came toward her. He dropped a kiss on her forehead and said, "Boris is in the calving stall."

Sarena sighed as he took off his jacket and hung it on a hook by the back door. "Thanks for doing that. I just hate that he won't stay in his pen. He's not going to be happy in there."

"Theo said he'd visit him tomorrow, just to appease you." Darren kicked off his boots, lifted his hat, and ran his fingers through his hair. He gave her a grin and added, "You'll probably be out there too."

"Probably," she said, though it was a definitely.

He joined her at the island counter and took some popcorn despite Sorrell's glare. "Y'all better get your house done quickly," she said. "I can't be feeding you forever."

"What?" Darren asked, looking from Sorrell to Sarena and back. "We can't keep eating dinner here?"

"We're going to starve," Sarena said, only half-teasing. She reached for more popcorn, and Sorrell swatted her hand with the wooden spoon she'd just gotten out.

"Stop eating that."

"You're just going to make more," Sarena said with a smile. "You have the spoon out already."

"You owe me," Sorrell said, turning to get out more microwave popcorn and the white chocolate bark from the pantry.

"Owe you what?" Sarena asked. "I don't have anything."

"You get to ask Seren what she's really been doing at night."

"No," Sarena said, actually horrified. "No, Sorrell, you're so much better at approaching difficult topics."

"You ate my popcorn."

Sarena looked helplessly at Darren. "What's going on with Seren?" he asked.

"She's sneaking around," Sarena said. "Maybe you could ask her about it."

He chuckled and shook his head. "I don't think so, sweetheart. But I do have something I wanted to talk to you about." He cut a look at Sorrell, who nodded.

"She's in on it?"

"A little," he said. "Do you have it?"

"Yes." Sorrell stepped over to the fridge and opened the top compartment in the door. "It's right here." She took something out and handed it to Darren, who'd stood up and joined her in the kitchen.

"What's going on?" Sarena asked.

"I don't need a big wedding," Darren said. "And I don't think you want one either. But I was thinking." He cleared his throat and set a black box on the counter. "That it would be nice to have my friends and family there. Just my parents and my siblings. Their families. Your aunts and cousins. The cowboys at Chestnut Ranch. Your cowboys here."

Sarena couldn't look away from the black box. It had a fancy, silver design etched into the velvet, and only women in movies got boxes like that.

"I love you, Sarena, and this is a real marriage. Maybe we

could do a vow renewal or something, and invite everyone. Maybe at our new place." He looked at Sorrell, who nodded and smiled encouragingly.

He picked up the box and rounded the island. He dropped to both knees, and Sarena's emotions surged. "Will you remarry me?" He cracked open the box to reveal a beautiful ring that glinted in the bright overhead lights. "This is your mother's wedding ring, from her wedding with your dad."

Sarena's eyes filled with tears, blurring the ring and her handsome husband's face. She started to nod, and Darren asked, "Yeah?"

"Yes," she said.

He got back on his feet and she stood up to hug him. With trembling fingers, she held out her left hand and let him slip the ring on. "I love you," he said.

"I love you too." She kissed him, well-aware of Sorrell's watchful eye.

"You two are so cute," she said, and Sarena broke the kiss, a smile spreading across her mouth.

Sorrell slammed the microwave, ending the moment, but Sarena's heart continued to vibrate in a very good way. "Nothing fancy," she said.

"You can wear the same dress," he said. "I don't care. I just think my parents would like to be there, and I know my oldest sister would be. My mother said she was *not* happy when she found out I'd gotten married again and hadn't told anyone."

"I'm sorry," Sarena said, because that was her fault.

"It's just Jan," Darren said. "She's dramatic. It's fine."

"So we'll have dinner," Sorrell said. "And a little ceremony here at the ranch. It'll be fun."

"Yeah," Darren said, smiling at Sarena. "Fun."

"Can't wait," Sarena said, though she didn't really want all those eyes on her. Everyone would know the first time she and Darren had gotten married hadn't been real.

They already know, she told herself, and it didn't matter anyway. The marriage was real to her, and real to Darren, and that was all that mattered.

"We'll set a date once we know when the house will be done," Darren said. "All right?"

"All right." She swayed with him, enjoying his presence in her house and her life. She liked the way he held her, and the way he smiled at her, and the way he loved her.

"Griffin's wedding is tomorrow," he said. "I said I'd go help set up, so I have to be over there at ten."

"It starts at eleven, right?" Sarena asked.

"Yep."

"I'll be there," she said. "If Seren doesn't kill me for asking her about her secret activities tonight."

Chapter 27

Darren set up chairs in neat rows, along with several other people. Aaron hadn't gotten the chair job, but Millie had asked him to come to her house and load up the food she'd been cooking for days.

Darren knew, because she'd been using him as a taste-tester for the past three weeks. He suspected it was because she wanted him to know how much the Johnson brothers valued him at Chestnut Ranch. But she'd never said anything, and she'd never asked him where he'd disappeared to over Thanksgiving.

She simply said, "I'm thinking of this for the main dish," as she put a plate of steak, yellow rice, and balsamic green beans in front of him. He'd eaten it all, and everything Millie touched tasted amazing.

He'd asked her why she didn't ask Griffin or Toni to taste the food, and she'd said they wanted to be surprised. Darren didn't care what he ate at his wedding dinner either, and he'd

accepted her answer. He'd enjoyed his time in Millie and
Travis's house, eating what Millie made and keeping his eye on
her while she cooked with her pregnant belly.

She was due in only a few weeks, and she'd told him she
couldn't wait until this wedding was over. Darren had thought
about asking her to plan the vow renewal for him and Sarena,
but he hadn't. Sorrell might get her feelings hurt, and really, all
they needed was some food—which Sorrell would provide.

Plus, they'd have a brand new house, and Darren didn't
need to hire a party planner.

He set out the chairs, and when those were done, he
looked for someone who would know what he should do next.

"Time to line up," Millie said. There were no bows on the
backs of the chairs. No misters blowing down from the deck
above the patio. Russ's wedding had been sweltering, and
Darren thought a winter wedding in Texas was the smartest
idea ever.

He turned to find Sarena, because he didn't need to line
up. He wasn't actually a member of the Johnson family,
though he sure did appreciate that they treated him like he
was. He found Conrad Johnson standing behind him, and he
grinned at the man. "Conrad." He shook the older gentle-
man's hand, noting that the cowboy still had plenty of grip
left. "Where's your wife?"

"She's helping Toni's mother. Help me up front?"

"Yes, sir." Darren steadied the man by putting his hand on
Conrad's elbow as they walked slowly down the aisle to the
front row. Conrad sighed as he sat down, and Darren gave him
a second to get settled.

He'd always liked Conrad, and he knew how hard it was for him to not be working on the ranch he'd shaped for so long.

"Thanks, Darren. Go find your wife."

"All right." Darren flashed him a smile and looked around for Sarena. He spotted her hanging out in the corner with her sisters and Janelle Stokes, and he made his way toward her. The Johnsons were a prominent, long-time family of Chestnut Springs, and it seemed like the entire town had turned up for the wedding of the last brother.

"We better sit down, or we won't have a seat," he said when he got to the girls. "And aren't you supposed to be lined up?" He looked at Janelle, who held the hand of one of her girls.

"Yeah, I suppose so," she said. "Millie's like a drill sergeant with the lining up." She gave them a healthy smile, and Darren knew she loved Millie despite her teasings. "Can you guys take the girls to their seats? We have some up front by Russ's parents."

"Sure," Sarena said, taking the little blonde girl's hand. Darren had never pictured himself taking care of children, but he sure did like the sight of Sarena doing it.

"Oh, it looks like Kelly is up there already," Janelle said. "Kade, you go with them and sit by your sister, okay?"

The girl nodded, and Sarena set out to deliver her where she needed to be. Then they sat down, taking the last four seats on the end of a row about halfway back, beside Brian and the other Chestnut Ranch cowboys. Soft music played from some speakers somewhere, and about ten minutes later, it quieted.

"Welcome to Chestnut Ranch," Griffin said, a heartiness in his voice that gave away his excitement. Darren couldn't see him, but he obviously had a mic somewhere.

"And welcome to Camp Clear Creek," Toni said, a giggle following.

"Thanks for coming to yet another party during the holidays," Griffin said. "We promise not to keep you too long."

"And we'll feed you well," Toni said. "Just like a good Texan does."

"So, if you'll all turn around, we'll get this done."

Darren twisted in his seat, but he didn't see anything on the patio. Someone said, "They're up on the deck," and he looked up to find Toni and Griffin standing right at the railing, both of them holding a microphone.

Several people aah'ed, and Darren smiled at his friend. Griffin had been through some hard things in his life, and it did Darren's heart and soul good to see him standing up on the deck like he was the King of England, waving down at his subjects.

He wore a smile the size of Texas, and a deep, dark tuxedo with an expensive cowboy hat. Toni wore a beautiful, long, white gown, and lifted her microphone to her mouth. "Fraternizing at Camp Clear Creek is technically against the rules."

"But I got special permission to see Toni," Griffin said. "At night, after hours, when no one else would see us."

"Oh, boy," Darren said, grinning. Beside him, Brian stiffened and pulled in a tight breath. Darren looked at him, but his eyes were glued to Griffin and Toni.

"We had our ups and downs," Toni said.

"And once, she pushed me in the lake."

"I did not," Toni said, laughing. "But Griffin did let his boys practically burn down the main building."

"I was not in charge during that episode," he said, shaking his head.

"Somewhere along the way, we fell in love," Toni said, her voice turning tight at the end.

"I don't want to do this at our vow renewal," Sarena whispered.

Darren reached over and took her hand, shaking his head. "Me either."

But this was right up Griffin's alley.

"For the record," Griffin said. "I'd been trying to get Toni to go out with me for two summers before this past one."

"He even kissed me at his brother's wedding, *before* camp started." Toni beamed at her husband-to-be.

"Persistence pays off," he said, and people in the crowd chuckled. "I love you, Toni. I've wanted to be yours for a long time, and I'm grateful it's happening today."

"I love you, too, Griffin. I can't wait to start our life together."

The pastor appeared in the scene, pronounced them man and wife, and took the microphones so Griffin could tip Toni back and kiss her.

The crowd erupted into cheers, mostly led by the loudest Johnson brother—Rex. Seth, Russ, and Travis didn't hold back either, and Darren clapped and hollered like everyone else.

"We will serve cake first," Toni said into one of the mics

the pastor still held. "And then dinner, because we don't want anyone to be too full for dessert."

"Can we do that?" Darren asked as people started standing up. "Have only desserts at our renewal?"

"Sure," Sarena said, but Sorrell asked, "You want only desserts at your vow renewal?" and made a face like she smelled something bad.

"I think that's a no," Darren said, smiling.

"It's just, I have the perfect wedding brunch planned," Sorrell said.

"Maybe you should do that at *your* wedding," Sarena said, and that earned her a glare from Sorrell.

"What?" Sarena asked. "I'm just saying. Serendipity is obviously sneaking around, probably seeing someone. You should text Theo and see what he's doing tonight."

"I am *not* sneaking around," Serendipity said, but Darren had listened to Sarena's stories last night while they lay in bed, and he definitely thought she was.

"Excuse me," Brian said, and he pushed past Darren, practically knocking a chair over as he went by. Darren watched him go, surprise moving through him. Brian was usually pretty chill, and that move was completely out of character.

"Stop badgering me about Theo," Sorrell said, and Darren refocused on the Adams sisters. "I'll go out with him when the time is right."

"A-ha!" Sarena squeezed his hand too tight and then let it go. When she stepped in front of Sorrell, her eyes were wide, bright, and hopeful. "You'll go out with him?"

"You're causing a scene," Sorrell hissed. "Come on. Let's get some cake and stop talking."

"Amen to that," Serendipity said, shooting a glare at Sarena. She marched away, and Darren wondered if his wife had pushed Serendipity just a bit too far. She hadn't admitted to anything, and Sarena had come to bed more frustrated than when the intervention had started.

On the patio, the newlyweds shook hands and gave hugs while people went through the line to get cake. Griffin grabbed onto Darren and hugged him tight, pounding him on the back.

"You did it," Darren said, stepping back and grinning at his friend.

"So did you," he said, glancing at Sarena. He smiled and smiled, the glow of happiness around him such an amazing thing to see.

"Congratulations," Darren said. "Married life is the best."

"He's right," Seth said, stepping into the circle. He hugged his brother, and so did Russ as congratulations went around.

Darren fed off their joy, taking it and matching his to it. He reached for Sarena's hand again and kept her close to him.

Later, after the cake, the dinner, and the dancing, Darren walked with her down the road a bit to the cowboy cabins, where he'd parked his truck earlier that day.

"Do you really think married life is the best?" she asked.

He looked at her, that contemplative look on her face he liked so much. "Yes," he said. "I'm the happiest I've ever been."

"Even more than when you were married to Diana?" She looked at him too, a vulnerability there that surprised Darren.

"Yes," he said. "Though I loved her, and I loved being married to her."

She nodded like she understood, but she couldn't. Darren barely did. "It's hard to describe. But I think the human heart and mind has an unlimited capacity to love. So while I did love her then, I'm completely and absolutely in love with you now. I love being married to you. I love being with you. I love that we're building a life and a future together."

"It's not going to be easy."

"No," he said. "Probably not." He reached to open her door. "Life is challenging. But I'd rather have someone at my side to experience it with."

"Me too," she said, stepping into his arms. "I want you, Darren Dumond."

"And I want you, Sarena Dumond." He kissed her, and she kissed him back, and yes, married life was absolutely amazing.

In **A COWBOY AND HIS SECRET KISS**, you'll get to see what happens with Brian and Serendipity, a ranch hand at Chestnut Ranch and one of the Adams sisters. Read on for a sneak peek!

Sneak Peek! Chapter One of A Cowboy and his Secret Kiss

Brian Gray sat on the end of the row, thinking that at least Darren and Sarena had splurged for comfortable seats. Darren had been living in the farmhouse at Fox Hollow Ranch for the last several months, but the house they'd been building had been finished last week.

After today's vow renewal, Brian would be staying with the other cowboys to help them move.

He didn't want to, just like he'd rather be anywhere but sitting in this chair—padded or not—on this deck. He hadn't trundled down the road to the farmhouse here for months, not that he'd done so much before either.

When he came to Fox Hollow, he only made it fifty feet down the dirt lane before he pulled over into the stand of trees that hid his truck from Serendipity's sisters. But he'd stopped doing that just before Christmas, when he'd finally told Seren that he couldn't keep sneaking around with her.

She'd actually seemed perplexed by him wanting to pick

her up at the front door. "I don't see why it matters," she'd said.

It mattered to Brian. When he'd asked her why she couldn't tell her sisters about their relationship—which had been seven weeks old at the time, and he still hadn't kissed her —she'd only blinked at him. Without a response, Brian had simply shook his head and added, "Sorry, Seren. That doesn't work for me."

The problem was, the past six months hadn't really been working for him either.

Serendipity Adams currently sat several rows in front of him, her back tall and straight, her dark hair curled, clipped back, and cascading over her shoulders. Brian's fingers fisted just thinking about touching that hair. He wanted to cradle her face in his palm, lean toward her, and kiss her.

He hadn't stopped thinking about doing just that for the past eight months. Eight long months of torture from within his own mind. He hadn't been this hung up on Cassie, his ex-wife, and he couldn't figure out why the idea of being with Serendipity wouldn't stop tormenting him.

The pastor stood at the edge of the deck now, and the back door opened behind Brian. He turned and stood, along with the rest of the small crowd. If he could've gotten away with not coming to this, he would have stayed at Chestnut Ranch. As it was, he hadn't been able to figure out how to tell Darren —and by doing that, Sarena—that he couldn't sit on this padded chair and watch the vow renewal.

He shifted his feet as Darren came outside, wearing a dark suit, a pure black cowboy hat, and a wide smile. He extended his hand to someone still inside, and Sarena put her hand in his and came outside. The crowd sighed as a single unit, and Brian could admit that she was simply stunning in a white dress that went over her shoulders with thick straps and fell all the way to the ground in long waves of lace.

She didn't carry flowers, and all of her adornments were simple. Gold hoop earrings, and no other jewelry. She wore makeup, but not so much that she looked like a different person. Seren was a lot like that, with a fresh face that floated through Brian's mind every night before he fell asleep.

Sarena linked arms with Darren, and together, they walked down the center aisle while some frilly music played out of the house. They reached the front of the crowd and stood before the pastor.

Brian's throat scratched, and the air going down felt like the wrong thing to breathe. He managed to sit along with everyone else, and someone closed the door to silence the music. Once everyone was settled, Pastor Hamilton said, "Welcome to everyone here today to witness the vow renewal of Darren Dumond and Sarena Adams."

He continued to lead them through a very simple ceremony, which ended five minutes later when Sarena finished saying how much she loved Darren and always wanted to be with him.

The crowd stood again, clapping and cheering this time. Brian played his part, though he couldn't find a trace of happiness in his body. At least not for himself. He did smile for Darren and Sarena, who'd managed to stay married for three times as long as Brian had.

He wondered if he'd ever get married again. At only thirty-five, he didn't want to think about spending the next forty years by himself. Darren had gotten himself a dog last year, and Brian had followed in his footsteps.

His German shepherd had run out onto the ranch when Brian had arrived with Tomas and Aaron, and he wished he had Queen at his side to calm him. The dog had been training to enter the police force, but she'd failed one of the tests. Brian had paid a lot of money for her, but everyone thought he'd rescued her from the animal shelter.

They didn't ask where he'd gotten her, and he hadn't told them. That was his policy. If no one asked specifically, he didn't tell. Then he didn't have to lie, and the policy had served him well for a long time.

"Okay," Sorrell said. Brian looked at the third Adams sister. "We're having brunch out here before we all help the happy couple move into their new home. I just need a few minutes to get it all set up." She turned to the two cowboys who worked at Fox Hollow, and the three of them hurried down the aisle and into the house.

The music spilled out the open doorway again, and Theo and Phillip set up two long tables that Sorrell proceeded to fill with flutes of champagne and orange juice, croissants, salmon and cream cheese bagel sliders, fresh fruit, and caramelized onion mini quiches.

Brian's mouth watered, but he hung back, because Seren flitted around the tables too, putting out silverware, plates, and napkins. He couldn't help watching her, and if she felt the weight of his gaze on her face, she never acknowledged it.

"All right," Sarena said, taking up a position in front of the tables and raising both arms. Darren stepped to her side, the glow of happiness on his face so obvious. "Thank you all for coming, not only to the renewal but to help us move." She grinned out at everyone. "And a special thank you to Sorrell, who singlehandedly made this brunch for us."

Both she and Darren beamed at Sorrell, and Theo started the applause for her. Sorrell's face flushed, but her smile gave away how pleased she was.

"Okay, let's eat," she finally said, shooting a look at Theo and Phillip. Neither of them looked ashamed or embarrassed though, and in fact, Theo grinned at Sorrell in a way that told everyone exactly how he felt about her. Anyone looking, anyway, and Brian was always looking.

He felt like a silent observer everywhere he went, and he wondered if it was time for him to move on. Find another ranch to work. He'd been at Chestnut Ranch for six years, and he'd spent a couple at another one just outside of Fredericksburg after his move from the Pacific Northwest.

One more glance at Serendipity, and Brian didn't want to move on. He wanted another chance with the tall, leggy brunette who'd somehow stolen his heart in a single second. Or maybe when she'd chased him down the lane to give him her number.

A number which he still had. A number he'd texted plenty of times in the past to ask her what time they could meet.

His hand immediately inched into his pocket, reaching for his phone. Maybe he could just text her now. Ask her again.

His throat constricted, and he swallowed, trying to find

the courage he needed to send such a text. He should definitely do it before he ate, he knew that much. In fact, he wasn't sure how he chew and swallow at all until the text had been sent, and yet, he didn't quite know the words to use.

"You comin'?" Aaron asked, and Brian's hand slipped right out of his pocket.

"Yeah," he said, following the other cowboy toward the tables near the house. Plenty of others had already gotten their food, and with the small crowd, it hadn't taken long. In front of him, Aaron picked up a plate and proceeded to put one of everything on it. Brian had heard about Sorrell's excellent skill in the kitchen from Seren, and he should want one of everything too.

He used the delicate tongs and tiny forks to do the same as Aaron, finally taking a mimosa to occupy his other hand. Then he couldn't text Seren, who'd taken her plate of food to one of the tables that someone had set up at some point. Brian hadn't seen when, and he wondered how long he'd stood there with his hand in his pocket, trying to decide if he could text Seren or not.

Still following Aaron, he sat at another table and put down his plate and drink. He didn't waste any time now as he swiftly reached for his phone and pulled it from his pocket. He swiped and tapped, typing out Seren's name and getting the message started.

I miss you. I'd love to maybe see if we can try again. Later today after Darren and Sarena are moved? Same spot as usual?

He stared at the words, wondering if they were too desperate. To make matters worse, he added *Tell me what time, and I'll be there,* and sent the whole thing. He wasn't sure if Seren had her phone with her, and he kept his eyes on her back as he picked up his quiche. At the table beside him, the Johnson brothers laughed loudly about something, and Brian knew he didn't want to leave Chestnut Ranch. He loved the land there, and he loved working with good men like them.

He wanted to talk to Seth about Serendipity, but he hadn't known how to bring it up. Seth had always been the brother to ask the most questions, but he'd been really distracted with the upcoming adoption he and Jenna were hoping would go through.

"This is amazing," he said, realizing what he'd just put in his mouth. The salty onions and creamy eggs melted in his mouth, and his appetite returned despite the silence of his phone. He'd just finished the delicious brunch when his phone buzzed.

"Just leave the dishes," Darren said in that moment. "We'll clean it all up later. We've got plenty of work for you to do." He laughed, and so did several others.

"Yeehaw!" Theo whooped, and that set off Rex, and then Griffin.

"Oh, boy," Aaron said, grinning. "He's got them going now."

"Boxes in the house," Darren said over the commotion. "We'll need the big muscles to move the furniture."

"So not you," Rex said, jostling Travis.

"Funny," Travis said back. "I'm pretty sure I'm stronger than you."

"Please," Rex said. "You don't even work the ranch anymore."

"I lift weights," Travis said. "And Porter is no lightweight." He grinned at Millie, his wife, who held their baby boy in her arms. He leaned over and kissed her adding, "You gonna head home, baby?"

"When Jenna goes," Millie said. "She's my ride."

Travis nodded, and he practically shoved Rex toward the back door. "Let's go, Strong Man. You can probably take the couch by yourself."

Rex said something in return, but the noise level had increased, and Brian couldn't hear what. He loved the relationship between the Johnson brothers, and how they'd always made him feel like part of them too. He missed his brother in that moment, though he hadn't spoken to Tom in a couple of months.

He made a mental note to call Tom, and he pulled out his phone to make the note physical. He couldn't keep his mental notes as straight as he once had, and time would slip away from him, and the next time he'd remember to call Tom would be late at night or while he was driving. Sometime when he couldn't do it, and then more days would pass.

The text notification at the top of the screen reminded him of the buzzing of his phone, and his heart vibrated along with it. His chest almost hurt as hope filled him. He pulled down from the top of his screen, and his breath caught in his throat.

Serendipity's name sat there, along with a short text. *4:30. I miss you too.*

Brian seized onto those words, and they echoed through his whole head. His ears, his mind, his chest. *I miss you too.*

"Are you going to stand there all day?" Seth asked, causing Brian to jump. He looked up and at Seth, who gazed at Brian's phone.

"No," Brian said, shoving his phone back into his pocket at the same time he stepped out of the doorway. "Sorry."

"Not a problem." Seth grinned at him. "But we better get a move on if you've got somewhere to be at four-thirty." He wore a glinting, knowing look in his eye as he grinned and stepped past Brian into the house.

Four-thirty. It seemed impossibly far away and yet way too close at the same time. "Yeah," he said. "We better."

Sneak Peek! Chapter Two of A Cowboy and his Secret Kiss

Serendipity Adams stuck to the lighter boxes as the activity around the farmhouse amped up. She could carry more, but there was no need as Darren had brought all of the cowboys from Chestnut Ranch to help with moving day.

Moving day.

She couldn't believe her sister was moving out. Seren reminded herself that Sarena wasn't going very far. Two hundred yards, as she'd been telling Sorrell for the past few weeks. Sorrell, the middle sister, was definitely having a hard time with their oldest sister's departure from the farmhouse than anyone else.

Seren bent to pick up another box, a groan coming out of her mouth. "This one's heavy," she said, though she wasn't talking to anyone specific.

"Let me."

Seren knew that voice. That voice haunted her when she

woke up each morning and followed her around while she led groups to the top of Enchantment Rock.

She managed to turn her head to look at Brian Gray, the handsome cowboy she'd started seeing last fall. Maybe it was winter, though Seren didn't think winter's cold kiss ever truly came to the Texas Hill Country. She absorbed the strong lines of his jaw, which sported a trim, neat, and very sexy beard in the brownish-blond hair that covered Brian's head too.

He had a lot of hair, and Seren never had touched it. *What a shame*, she thought to herself as they continued to stare at one another.

He'd texted her a couple of hours ago and then promptly gotten to work moving the bed, the new couches Darren and Sarena had bought for their new house, and more after she'd responded to his message. He hadn't said anything back, and Seren told herself again that he didn't need to.

He'd asked to see her, and she'd agreed. Given him a time. They'd never done more than that before unless they had something fun or important to say to one another.

Brian's dark eyes devoured her, and Seren couldn't believe she hadn't allowed herself to kiss him last time. He'd wanted to kiss her. He'd even tried once before she'd told him she wasn't ready.

The truth was, Seren might never be ready to kiss a man like Brian Gray. She never had kissed someone like him before, and as soon as his lips touched hers, he'd know that. In fact, Seren had only kissed two other men before, and neither of them were all that memorable.

Besides the fact that the last cowboy who'd taken his hat

off to kiss her had laughed afterward. That had definitely burned itself into her memory, and her throat tightened at the nearness of Brian.

The scent of his cologne entered her nose, and he called to her in a way no one else ever had. He'd been working for a while in the June heat, and he reached up and removed his hat. Her heart went into overdrive, her pulse moving through her ribcage and down into her organs.

He wiped his forehead with a towel and reseated his hat. Of course he wasn't going to kiss her right now. The very idea was absolutely ridiculous.

"I can get it," he said. "Your sister said there were a few boxes in here with books." He lifted the box as if it held feathers and added, "Yep, this is one of those." He nodded at her and turned around.

She watched him walk away, a flush of heat moving through her whole body. His biceps strained, so the box actually was heavy. But wow. Seren sure did like the way his jeans hung off his hips and the way his dark gray T-shirt strained across his wide shoulders.

All of the cowboys had changed after the vow renewal and following brunch. It had been a wonderful ceremony, and Seren was glad Sarena had gotten the event she wanted. She'd bought another dress for this ceremony, though she'd purchased one for the fake wedding they'd held at Fox Hollow last October.

Darren, apparently, had a lot of money. He'd funded the new house two hundred yards down the lane too, which he'd also paid to extend to their front driveway. They hadn't removed any trees, as the land conservation was important to Sarena—and to Seren too.

"Almost done in here," Darren said, entering the office where Seren still stood, mute. He bent and picked up another box, groaning under the weight of it. "Why did she put so much in one box?" He gave Seren a dark look and followed Brian out of the room and then the house.

With only a couple of boxes left, and with Seren assuming they also held books, she decided to leave them there for the cowboys to take. She went down the hall and into the back of the house, where the kitchen and living room spread before her.

Sorrell worked there, rinsing dishes and setting them in the dishwasher. Darren had replaced that too, for Sorrell's birthday. Her sister had burst into tears and hung onto his neck while she hugged him. Theo had brought her flowers and her favorite hazelnut chocolates and asked her to dinner.

Seren wasn't sure if her sister had said no or not, but she knew the date hadn't happened yet. She'd always believed it would, but she was starting to have her doubts. At the same time, she'd thought she'd ruined whatever chance she and Brian had, but he'd still texted.

Theo himself walked through the back door at that moment, and said, "Sorrell, this is all there is." He carried dishes and glasses in both hands and walked them over to the sink where Sorrell stood. She was the lightest of the Adams sisters, with hair the color of taupe that she actually lightened with an at-home dye kit. Her eyes bore the color of milk chocolate cocoa, and she glanced at Theo as he set the clinking dishes next to the sink.

"Thank you, Theo," she said, and Seren knew she'd been crying.

Thankfully, Theo stayed at her side, even putting his hand on her lower back as they worked at the sink together. Seren felt frozen to the spot as she watched them. She'd seen her mother and father doing a dance like this before, but it had been a very long time. She remembered the feeling of love and comfort as her father had looked at her mother, a glow of adoration on his face.

If Seren could see Theo's face, she was sure she'd see that same emotion on his face. She was glad he was there for Sorrell, as Seren didn't really understand her sister's emotions. Sometimes Seren felt like she was broken, as she didn't seem to think or feel things the same way other women did.

Because of that, she didn't have a whole lot of female friends. She barely had any friends at all. She'd always been close to her sisters, and for her, that was all she'd needed.

She was friends with her boss, Meg, though they didn't exactly have friendly lunches or go to movies outside of their work at the Enchantment Rock State Park.

Koda, Darren's dog came through the back door too, his tongue lolling out of his mouth. Seren sprang into action to get the canine something to drink. She'd found the presence of Koda at the farmhouse soothing and wanted. They'd never had a dog that lived inside and slept on the couch or the beds.

But Koda did. If he got too dirty outside on the ranch with

either Darren or Sarena, Darren just hosed him down on the back deck and then toweled him off before he let him inside. Seren loved the golden retriever, and she'd taken him to work with her several times, keeping him on the leash as she led her groups up the rock. Koda was a Rockstar, and he did whatever Seren told him to do.

She'd been seriously considering getting a dog of her own, after Sarena and Darren moved and took Koda with them.

"Hey, Koda," she said to the animal. He wore a smiling face, as he always did, and Seren brushed the dust from his long, golden hair. "Let me get you a drink."

Theo and Sorrell shifted, but Seren said, "I'll get a bottle."

"He's a dog," Sorrell said. "He doesn't need bottled water."

Seren ignored her, because of course Koda needed bottled water. She took two bottles out of the fridge and opened them to pour into the clean bowl she then collected from the cupboard.

"Don't use a bowl we eat out of," Sorrell said while Theo started chuckling.

"I'll wash it," Seren said, though she wouldn't. She'd load it into the dishwasher, though, if there was room after Sorrell got all the brunch dishes inside.

"You will not," Sorrell said, but Seren still set it on the floor and poured the two bottles of water into it.

A German shepherd came trotting inside the house too, and Seren paused at the magnificent sight of him. The dog had a glorious fawny coat, with all the characteristic black markings of a purebred German shepherd. "Oh, hello," she said. "And who are you?"

"That's Brian's dog," Theo said over his shoulder. "Her name's Queen."

Seren's heart bumped around inside her chest, quickly becoming dislodged as she bent down to greet the dog. "Come get something to drink, Queen."

Queen—and the dog clearly knew she was royalty. Brian probably treated her like one too, as she clearly came inside houses. She probably slept in his bed and on his couches too. *Lucky dog*, she thought, surprised at the thought. She'd barely kissed a man. Doing more than that...Seren gasped for a breath of the right substance to breathe.

The shepherd let her stroke her face and then she bent down and drank with Koda. The two of them lapped with their big tongues until they were satisfied, and then they both went over to the couches in the living room and jumped up on the biggest ones.

Seren loved them both so much, and she almost wished she didn't. She should want to spend her time with people she could speak with, not dogs who could keep her feet warm while she ate ice cream and rested her muscles from her long day at work.

To her right, Sorrell giggled, drawing Seren's attention. She looked at her and Theo again, a new idea growing and growing. The seed had been planted months ago, when Sarena, in another of her meddling attempts, had confronted Sorrell about going out with Theo.

She'd questioned Seren relentlessly about where she went at night too, and Seren had managed to put her off and say she wasn't sneaking around with anyone. She wasn't. Brian picked her up at the visitor's center or down the lane, and they went to dinner and movies. Just because it didn't happen in Chestnut Springs didn't mean she was sneaking.

She was keeping Brian a secret, because Sorrell had made her promise not to let a cowboy steal her heart and give it back to her in pieces. Seren had never had anyone, cowboy or not, coming knocking on her door, anxious for a date, so she'd agreed. She'd been able to keep the promise for years. Almost a decade. It had been easy, because the disastrous kiss with the Laughing Cowboy had happened a couple of months before.

She hadn't told anyone about it, not even her sisters. It was bad enough that Pierce's friends all knew. That everyone at the party knew. That she'd had to live through the humiliation the first time. She couldn't stand the thought of telling the story to anyone, least of all Sorrell, who would expect Seren to cry so she could stroke her hair and reiterate the fact that all cowboys had trouble running through their veins.

Seren hadn't cried. Not even once. Not over Benjamin Thrombey. He'd left town a couple of years later, and Seren lived and worked far enough from Chestnut Springs that she hadn't had to work too hard to steer clear of him or his friends.

Seren couldn't remember the last time she'd cried at all.

She tore her eyes from Sorrell and Theo, still dancing around each other in front of the sink. "I'm going to go shower," she said. "Get this dust and sweat off me."

"Okay," Sorrell said. "It was a great ceremony, wasn't it?"

Seren put a bright smile on her face, because she agreed with her sister. "Yes," she said. "It was."

"I still can't believe she's not going to come down the hall in the morning, ready for her coffee." She sniffled, and Seren took that as her cue to get out of there. As she walked away, Theo said something in a low voice, and Seren hoped Sorrell would just let go already.

Let go, and let herself go out with Theo. Let go, and let herself fall all the way in love with him.

Then maybe Seren could bring Brian out of the shadows and date him openly, the way he wanted.

Maybe, she thought, quickly switching her thoughts to a prayer. *Please, Dear Lord. If Sorrell can get out of her own way, then I can date Brian the right way. Please.*

She didn't want to hurt him. In fact, the idea of that made her physically ill. She may not think herself all that emotional, but she was considerate. She'd already hurt him, and Seren couldn't stand the thought of doing it again.

"Maybe you shouldn't meet him this afternoon." Seren showered quickly without washing her hair. Properly deodorized and dressed in a cute pair of black shorts and a white tank top. Though she rarely wore sandals around the ranch due to the amount of dust, today, she slipped on a strappy pair of flat sandals. She never wore heels, as she was already the tallest Adams sister.

With Brian, she could wear the extra height, because he stood much taller than her that heels wouldn't even touch. She didn't even own heels though, and she would never be able to walk in them. Since she'd already made a fool of herself in front of Brian—more than once—she was sticking to the flat sandals.

She'd thought about how she'd run after his truck after they'd met for the first time. She'd seen him around before, but they'd truly met when he'd come to help Darren move into the farmhouse.

Then she'd rejected his kiss, which only added another layer of embarrassment. Then she'd refused to let him come to the door to pick her up. Wouldn't go out with him unless they ate in another town. When he'd finally broken up with her, Seren had actually been relieved. Then she didn't have to keep adding more guilt to her gut. More embarrassment to what she already carried on a daily basis.

But maybe...

At four o'clock, the house seemed to be empty. Both dogs were gone, which meant Brian and Darren had come to get them at some point while she'd been hiding in her bedroom. She thought the farmhouse would probably feel and be a lot emptier now that Sarena and Darren and Koda didn't live here anymore. She clenched her teeth and stuffed her feelings back down into her stomach. She would be okay. Sarena deserved a home of her own, with the husband she loved. They wanted a family, and they needed a place of their own to raise that family.

Seren opted to walk down the dirt lane to the alcove of trees where she and Brian had met over the weeks they'd been seeing each other. She'd never arrived first, but she did today. Maybe things would be different this time.

You have to do something different to get a different result, she thought, unsurprised when she heard the rumble of an engine only a few minutes after she'd arrived.

Sure enough, Brian pulled his shiny, white truck around the corner a moment later. She tucked her hands in her back pockets and stayed out of the way while he parked. He got out, and still Seren felt like she was standing on wooden legs.

"Hey," he said, closing the door behind him.

The sun shone down, nice and warm, and Seren's nerves fired harshly. "Hey."

"So, um, do you want to go for a walk? Or should we stay here?" He looked around at the fully leafed trees, a smile crossing his face. "It looks different now that it's summer." When he met her gaze again, he wore a smile on his face.

"Let's stay here," Seren said, pushing her anxiety back. *Do something different.*

"All right." Brian nodded toward the back of his truck, where they'd sat and talked in the past. Before he could take too many steps, Seren darted in front of him. "Oh."

She looked into those eyes she liked so much, reaching up slowly. She traced her fingertips down the side of his face, that beard even more beautiful against her skin than she'd imagined.

Brian pulled in a slow breath, and Seren looked into his eyes. She wanted to ask him if he'd laugh. Or if he still wanted to kiss her. By the look in his eye, he did.

Because of that, Seren didn't waste another second. She tipped up onto her toes as she curled her other hand around the back of his neck, his fingers seeking out and finding that thick hair she'd dreamt about.

"Serendipity," he whispered, but she didn't know what to say. She had nothing to say. Her eyes drifted closed as Brian moved. He clearly knew what he was doing when it came to kissing a woman, because he put one hand on her waist while simultaneously using the other to remove his cowboy hat.

He leaned down and met her mouth with his, finishing the task she'd started. Seren sucked in a breath, her pulse positively pounding now. As if it hadn't been before. She had no idea what she was doing, but Brian obviously did. She felt treasured and adored as he kissed her and kept her close to him.

So Seren did what she hoped Sorrell would—she let go. She let go, and she enjoyed the way Brian kissed her. Wow, how he kissed her...

Ooh, find out what's going to happen with Serendipity and Brian in this secret relationship novel. **You can read A COWBOY AND HIS SECRET KISS in paperback!**

Chestnut Ranch Romance

Book 1: A Cowboy and his Neighbor: Best friends and neighbors shouldn't share a kiss...

Book 2: A Cowboy and his Mistletoe Kiss: He wasn't supposed to kiss her. Can Travis and Millie find a way to turn their mistletoe kiss into true love?

Book 3: A Cowboy and his Christmas Crush: Can a Christmas crush and their mutual love of rescuing dogs bring them back together?

Book 4: A Cowboy and his Daughter: They were married for a few months. She lost their baby...or so he thought.

Book 5: A Cowboy and his Boss: She's his boss. He's had a crush on her for a couple of summers now. Can Toni and Griffin mix business and pleasure while making sure the teens they're in charge of stay in line?

Book 6: A Cowboy and his Fake Marriage: She needs a husband to keep her ranch...can she convince the cowboy next-door to marry her?

Book 7: A Cowboy and his Secret Kiss: He likes the pretty adventure guide next door, but she wants to keep their relationship off the grid. Can he kiss her in secret and keep his heart intact?

Book 8: A Cowboy and his Skipped Christmas: He's been in love with her forever. She's told him no more times than either of them can count. Can Theo and Sorrell find their way through past pain to a happy future together?

Bluegrass Ranch Romance

Book 1: Winning the Cowboy Billionaire: She'll do anything to secure the funding she needs to take her perfumery to the next level...even date the boy next door.

Book 2: Roping the Cowboy Billionaire: She'll do anything to show her ex she's not still hung up on him...even date her best friend.

Book 3: Training the Cowboy Billionaire: She'll do anything to save her ranch...even marry a cowboy just so they can enter a race together.

Book 4: Parading the Cowboy Billionaire: She'll do anything to spite her mother and find her own happiness...even keep her cowboy billionaire boyfriend a secret.

Book 5: Promoting the Cowboy Billionaire: She'll do anything to keep her job...even date a client to stay on her boss's good side.

Book 6: Acquiring the Cowboy Billionaire: She'll do anything to keep her father's stud farm in the family...even marry the maddening cowboy billionaire she's never gotten along with.

Book 7: Saving the Cowboy Billionaire: She'll do anything to prove to her friends that she's over her ex...even date the cowboy she once went with in high school.

Book 8: Convincing the Cowboy Billionaire: She'll do anything to keep her dignity...even convincing the saltiest cowboy billionaire at the ranch to be her boyfriend.

Texas Longhorn Ranch Romance

Book 1: Loving Her Cowboy Best Friend: She's a city girl returning to her hometown. He's a country boy through and through. When these two former best friends (and ex-lovers) start working together, romantic sparks fly that could ignite a wildfire... Will Regina and Blake get burned or can they tame the flames into true love?

Book 2: Kissing Her Cowboy Boss: She's a veterinarian with a secret past. He's her new boss. When Todd hires Laura, it's because she's willing to live on-site and work full-time for the ranch. But when their feelings turn personal, will Laura put up walls between them to keep them apart?

About Emmy

Emmy is a Midwest mom who loves dogs, cowboys, and Texas. She's been writing for years and loves weaving stories of love, hope, and second chances. Find out more at www.emmyeugene.com.

Printed in Great Britain
by Amazon

15009619R00171